JB OR THE UNEXPECTED VIRTUE OF BEING SWAGGY

Also by J.T. Holden

Fiction
The Winter White House
True Son
Apple-polisher
Three Imaginary Boys
The Boys From Manchester

Poetry
Alice in Verse: The Lost Rhymes of Wonderland
Twilight Tales: A Collection of Chilling Poems
O the Dark Things You'll See!

JB

OR THE UNEXPECTED VIRTUE OF BEING SWAGGY

J.T. HOLDEN

[FEAT. KID SWAGGY]

KURO
黒

ISBN 13: 978-1-937696-17-7 • ISBN 10: 1937696170

First Edition

for Becky
for keeping my id in check

in memory of innocence,
before everything went viral

CONTENTS

PROLOGUE

I sometimes like to indulge in this little fantasy where I pretend that I cannot recall the first time I laid eyes on JB. I imagine it being this one time at the aquarium where the two of us appeared to be standing on opposite sides of the huge tropical fish display whose thick glass walls seemed to go on forever, as if their sole purpose was to keep us apart. Other times I imagine that I first saw him on that warm and sunny day at the beach where JB raced along the sand, his delightful laughter ringing through the bright summer sky as the gentle tide licked at his bare feet. Or possibly it was that chilly Halloween night when JB walked down the mirrored tunnel of the haunted house all by himself (even back then, he was a pretty determined kid, and he wasn't about to let the other kids see the fear that had coiled around his heart like a cold serpent; he simply stepped forward and entered the gaping mouth of the giant clown head, and kept on going until he reached the exit). Or maybe it was the day JB stood at the wishing well, with his eyes closed as he waited to hear his coin hit the water far below—maybe it was in that breathless moment of clarity just before he opened his eyes—maybe *that* was when I'd first caught sight of him.

Though all of these are very real memories and make

wonderful fodder for my fervid imagination, I am fully aware that my acquaintance with JB reaches much farther back than the aquarium, the beach, the haunted house, or the wishing well. Indeed we've known one another since time out of memory, and our connection runs far deeper than mere acquaintanceship.

Of course, none of that really matters.

What *does* matter is this: I believed in JB before *anyone* believed in JB—including JB *himself*.

And mine was a *true* belief from the very beginning. Not the fickle fancy of some screaming fangirl (or fanboy, of whom there are more than you'd think, trust me). And my impact on JB has easily been greater than that of anyone else. You might even say that I was his *de facto creator* . . . or at the very least, the model upon which the masterpiece was based. You could even go so far as to say that without me, there never would have *been* a JB . . . at least not as you know him today.

Legend has it that Frankenstein pondered for years before stitching together his creation and breathing life into it—an arduous and lengthy process which brought nothing but despair and death to his doorstep. Conversely, breathing life into *my* creation took only three days—with no blood, no body parts, and no worries of retribution. Having a complete lack of compunction in just about any given situation, there is little that I fear and nothing I won't do to get what I want. I am the ultimate supercilious *id*, and I have *never* let anything or anyone stand in my way when it comes to attaining whatever it is my heart desires. That's just the way I am.

Before I go on with my story, I would like to clear up one thing. It may seem like an insignificant detail to those who've already made up their minds, but to me, it is monumentally significant—indeed, it is the purpose of this book—and I would like to set the record straight once and for all.

Recently there have been rumors floating around the Web that JB disappeared for three days—and further, that he was abducted. While the former is true (JB did in fact disappear and wasn't heard from for three days), the latter is patently false. Contrary to popular belief, I did not abduct JB. I did not put a gun to his head. I did not use physical force. I did not threaten him in any way whatsoever. Nor did I use my considerable powers of persuasion to coerce him into coming with me on our little three-day adventure.

He came of his own free will—and his decision to do so was based in no small part on the intolerably suffocating influences of those surrounding him—friends, family, fans, and foes alike. He came with me to escape the box that *you*, dear readers, placed him in. So, if your finger is itching, please find the nearest reflective surface and point it in the right direction. I'm not here to apologize for anything I've done. *My* conscience is clear.

There was no abduction, no foul play, and no resistance from JB.

Of course, I am, after all, me, and so I suppose it's only fair that I shoulder *some* small measure of the "blame," if that's what you'd like to call it. But can I really be held any more accountable for the magnetism that drew JB to me than JB himself can be held accountable for the magnetism that drew all of you to him? That would be a bit like blaming the flame for the moth's inability to resist its radiance.

I suppose some bleeding hearts would snuff out such a flame just to spare a few wings getting singed. But where would we all be then? Cold and in the dark. And who wants that? I say let someone else worry about the moths while I bask in the warmth and brilliance of the raging fire. But then, that's just me, and I believe we've already established what *my* priorities are.

So anyway, on to the greater point, which I'm sure has you breathless with anticipation. Otherwise, you'd have already chucked this book and told me to slag off (which I can't say I'd blame you for, not in the least, because as hard as it may be for you to believe, sometimes even *I* get tired of hearing my shit).

But you may want to stick around for a while. Especially if you want to know about all this "abduction" crap that everybody in JB's trusted circle worked so hard to cover up at the time. And they did a good job of it too. Not one word in the press, not even so much as a blurb on a blog or a peep from Twitter. They just swept it under the carpet and acted like nothing happened.

I have to admit, at first I was like, *WTF?* I mean, come on, if Nick Jonas or Nick Tangorra (or even one of those geriatric boy band guys, like Nick Carter or Nick Lachey) had gone missing for even a *single* day, the Internet would have probably crashed with all the blogging and posting and reposting of a zillion people asking a zillion questions and offering another *ten* zillion speculations and hypotheses and all sorts of other crap. But when *the* most famous teen pop star on the face of the planet disappears for *three whole days*, we get nothing but the sound of crickets. Now tell me that isn't a cover-up!

Okay, JB *did* leave a note saying that he needed to get away and spend some time alone (how he managed *that* little maneuver without my knowledge is beyond me, but in any case, I didn't discover his betrayal until later; had I known about it at the time, I'd have slapped him silly—I mean, really, what's the point in a famous person going missing if it doesn't send the world into a tailspin?). But still, you'd have thought *somebody* in the golden circle would have leaked the story that the swaggy little prince had escaped the ivory tower without his entourage of bodyguards and cronies.

Hell, even Letterman kept his big mouth shut, and *he* knew all about it because when JB didn't show up for a scheduled appearance on *The Late Show*, Scooter called Letterman personally to explain the situation (Scooter is JB's manager, as those of you who've followed JB's career closely already know).

At first, Scooter didn't want to tell Letterman anything. He wanted to keep the whole incident in-house and pretend that everything was normal. And for good reason. He was worried about the media frenzy (and worse, the crazed fan frenzy) that would erupt if word of JB's disappearance got out. And with JB missing his scheduled spot on *The Late Show*, Scooter was doubly worried that Letterman might start making jokes about "JB MIA" and inadvertently spark the curiosity and overactive imaginations of both fans *and* the press, which would have most certainly led to a shitstorm of biblical proportions. Scooter could just see it: hordes of teenage girls taking to the streets, demanding that he produce JB. He could see paparazzi, press, and fans alike (and perhaps even a few shadier individuals who would love to get their hands on JB without his bodyguards there to protect him) scouring every corner of the planet in search of the prize. And images like these creeping into his thoughts made Scooter very uncomfortable. So he appealed to Letterman on behalf of JB's safety, and Letterman, who has always genuinely liked JB, held his tongue.

Even after JB had returned and made his "mea culpa" appearance on *The Late Show*, Letterman said nothing about the disappearance incident. Not even one joke. He didn't even ride JB for missing the previously scheduled interview. Pretty much all Letterman did was tease the kid about his new haircut and tattoo. Well, he also milked this huge laugh from the audience when JB mistakenly referred to the Sistine Chapel as the "Sixteenth Chapel." JB recovered from that little *faux pas* and continued with the interview, but I'll never forget the look of confusion bleeding into embarrassment on his face, which made it painfully clear that he was the only one *not* in on the joke. I sort of hated Letterman for having fun at the kid's expense. But I also respected him for keeping his word to Scooter and not revealing what he knew about the disappearance, even after JB was home and safe and it no longer mattered. I had to respect Letterman for that. And I had to respect

Scooter for the way he'd handled the whole thing with such a calm and level head.

I know that Scooter only had JB's best interests at heart. I know that his number one priority was to keep the kid safe from all the dangers that lurk outside in the real world. But there was one thing Scooter and all the others in the trusted circle hadn't considered in their grand effort to keep a lid on the story. Something more dangerous than any rabid fan or wacko nut job out there—with the obvious exception, of course, of that nutbag in the New Mexico State penitentiary, who, a few months after the Letterman interview, hired a couple of thugs to kidnap JB and do things to him that I won't even mention here (if you're the type of person who just can't live without knowing all the grisly little details, go Google the story—but fair warning: it was some pretty sick shit that freaky fan had planned for our hero) . . . and all because JB didn't respond to a fan letter! Can you believe that shit? Thankfully, *that* psycho fan's plot was foiled.

But back to my original point. The one danger that nobody had thought about or counted on was *me*.

Of course, this came as no surprise to yours truly—I am, after all, both wily and resourceful. And with my special "inside track" connection to JB (not to mention my sweet swaggy stealthy moves), no one—including JB himself—ever saw me coming.

THE NIGHT BEFORE

The night before his scheduled appearance on Letterman, JB couldn't get to sleep. He stayed up late, watching TV and playing video games, but he was far too restless to concentrate on either. He kept fidgeting in his seat and getting up like he was going to walk away and do something else, but then he would sit right back down and start flipping through channels—and when he couldn't find anything to hold his attention, he would reach for the game controller again. He was playing this old-school martial arts game that he didn't even care for that much when his drifting attention caused him to hit the wrong button, and his avatar took a crushing death blow and crumpled like a rag doll. This alone wouldn't have been so bad, but when his opponent flexed his muscles and roared this deep throaty chuckle through the surround speakers, JB's eyes went dark, and he whipped the controller at the screen.

It was an anticlimactic moment because the cord between the game unit and the controller wasn't long enough for the controller to make it to the TV's screen—it fell several inches shy of the mark before recoiling and falling to the carpet with a feeble thud. This only fueled JB's temper all the more, and he kicked the game unit hard enough to crack it but not enough to break it, and so the taunting laughter continued to emanate from the speakers while the words "K.O." and "YOU LOSE!" appeared in huge letters across the screen. For a moment, you would have almost sworn that he was going to put the heel of his shoe through the TV—or break every bone in his foot trying—but let's face it, that's really more *my* way of dealing with frustration, and he was still waiting on me to make my appearance, so he went outside to sit by the infinity pool and cool off.

It was a pleasant night, with a gentle breeze that soothed his burning cheeks and quenched his thirst for fresh air as he gazed at the shadows of the hills in the distance. It was the sort of night we had enjoyed together on numerous occasions before anyone ever knew who JB was. Just the two of us lying under the stars, dreaming of a time when *everyone* would know *exactly* who he was.

Well, maybe JB had other thoughts. Thoughts of being a normal kid with an average life—he's said as much in his book, and I have no reason to doubt his sincerity (if you know anything about JB, you know that, if nothing else, he is terminally sincere).

But for me, being "normal" and living some mundane existence in some podunk town was never an option. For me, it was the fame and fortune I saw gleaming in those stars . . . and the fans and the paparazzi and all the world chasing after JB with adoration, all of them wanting a piece of him, to touch him, or just to see him up close. I wanted the fast cars, designer clothes, and all the bling that comes as part and parcel of the star in ascension. I wanted the extravagant house on the hill with the stunning view and the shimmering infinity pool. I wanted all that and more. And I could see it in the stars on every single one of those nights we lay gazing up at the infinite sky, the two of us as one, like an explorer drifting in space.

I'm not ashamed to say what JB would never dare admit. I hated our childhood. I hated that we had next to nothing and that we had to survive mostly on the kindness and hand-me-downs of others. I hated that our "parentals"—and I use that term loosely—were as messed up as they were. If you think that sounds like a bit of a harsh assessment, spend a couple of hours at the age of two waiting on the front stoop for your old man to pick you up, only to discover that he's not coming . . . overhear someone recounting the story of how your mom smashed a beer bottle into your old man's teeth (justifiably so) and how, with blood dripping from his mouth, your old man called her every name in the book . . . witness a fight that ends with your mom kicking your old man in the family jewels, and after he recovers from the pain, your old man spits on your mom then grabs you and stuffs you into a snowsuit while your mom begs him not to take you . . . live through some crazy shit like that and then tell me how harsh you think my assessment of the old parentals is.

So, yeah, I pretty much hated everything about our life back then. And I'm absolutely positive that if not for my indomitable influence, we would still be there. And I'm certainly not about to apologize for that.

Anyway, back to my point: I knew early on the sort of life I wanted to live, and in my mind (or at least my little corner of *JB's* mind) I had resolved that nothing was going to stand in my way.

It has been said—by no less than Freud himself in his Structural Model of the Psyche—that I am driven solely by the "pleasure principle" and that if all of my needs, wants, and desires are not met with immediate satisfaction, I will throw a tantrum and display destructive behavior.

And this is true.

Though, admittedly, this "pleasure principle" was a far more acute trait *before* JB turned three—a pivotal moment in our development—because up until then, I pretty much had complete control over any given situation; the sort of control that kings and gods can only dream of.

But as time passed and JB grew, things changed, and I had

to devise and employ more *delicate*—and decidedly crafty—methods of persuasion to get my way (which was no small task for someone as profoundly self-focused and rigidly inflexible as I). The most notable changes coincided with the appearance of my "brothers"—the other two components of old Freud's Structural Model of the Psyche: the *ego* and *superego*—or as I called them: Lil E and Super E.

Now Lil E wasn't all that bad; he actually helped me get a grasp on reality and rein in the old wild spirit (at least to a slightly more acceptable degree), and he never interfered with my pursuit of pleasure. He even helped me to get what I wanted with less effort by teaching me how to use my innate talents—chief among them, my canny ability to bring a mischievous grin to JB's lips while simultaneously working his puppy dog eyes to melt the heart (and resolve) of just about any adult. As reserved as he was, Lil E knew how to work the old charm, and he was a masterful instructor to whom I am forever indebted for teaching me the fine art of emotional extortion.

Super E, however, was a completely different sort of entity. Far more complex than either Lil E or I, Super E quickly became the sunny yang to my shadowy yin.

Super E showed up when JB turned five, and nothing was quite the same after. Obsessed with rules and morals, and filled with a sense of righteousness that would have choked even the most devout of saints, Super E was like that officious little narc the teacher leaves in charge of the class when she steps out of the room. His patience was infuriating, and his manners made me physically sick (I'm serious, there were times when I actually felt like vomiting right there inside JB's brain). Super E was literally obsessed with doing the right thing, and he actually believed that personal sacrifice was *good* for you! Can you believe that?

I would have just taken the little prick out if it weren't for the fact that he was so strong. I'm talking Hulk vs. Thor strong here. I suppose there was a time, early on, when I could have crushed Super E like a grape—back when he wasn't so super, you know? But in truth, he sort of fascinated me—at least at the beginning, he did. I'd never seen anything like him. He was like this golden light gleaming on the horizon of JB's consciousness, like some mildly hypnotic force that didn't seem even remotely threatening—a force that in fact almost seemed like destiny, or providence, rising to make everything better . . . to make everything the way it *should* be. And for a while there, I truly believed in Super E. Or at least a small part of me did—but let's face it, that might have just been Lil E tugging at my sleeve like a doe-eyed kid (he does that on occasion, and I'm ashamed of how many times it's worked on me). And by the time I'd finally got my head straight and realized that Super E was just an interloping usurper (much like all the so-called "friends and family" who often come crawling out of the woodwork when a "loved one" becomes a superstar), it was too late. Super E was there to stay. And with Lil E refusing to take sides, I was on my own.

This in itself wasn't all that bad. I generally prefer to go it solo anyway (having to work with either of my "brothers of the Psyche" can be a real chore, and I liked it much better when it was just me and JB).

What *was* bad—scratch that—what was *completely miserable and intolerable* was this: JB and Super E began to meld into one! Not one as in "a couple of inseparable friends," like JB and I used to be. I mean *one*, as in the *same* person! It was as if JB had *absorbed* Super E and together they formed a whole new person—one that I scarcely recognized. And what really galled me was that it had happened so *quickly*. One minute they were hanging out in the distant regions of JB's consciousness, while I was kicked aside like an old toy that JB had outgrown, and the next they were like those twins on that teen werewolf show on MTV, melded into a single powerful entity, indistinguishable from their former selves because they were no longer *separate*. They were now one and the same—the "new and improved" JB.

To be honest, the new JB *did* have some undeniable pluses. He was gentle and sweet and kind, and when he smiled, it would light up this place in your soul that you didn't even know existed. And at the risk of sounding completely corny, whatever it was inside of him that shined out from that smile, it not only made him special; it had the power to make you *believe*.

Now don't get me wrong here. It's not like old Super E moved in and took control overnight. While his eventual "melding" with JB happened in a virtual flash, Super E's "development" took place over the course of years—so many in fact that I'm a little embarrassed to admit how long it took me to figure out that the special bond Super E had formed with JB was actually something I could use to my advantage . . . if and when I could ever worm my way back in, that is. But for a time, I was uncertain, thinking only of my impending doom.

So while JB's star was on the rise, I had to acclimate to life on the periphery, carefully picking and choosing when to assert myself, though never with full force. I'm a realist (thanks mostly to Lil E); I knew the score. Besides, with JB's newly enhanced strength developing rapidly by the day (thanks entirely to Super E), it would have been pointless for me to attempt forcing the scales back into my favor. Waiting and watching was the only viable option.

I'm not going to lie and tell you that I knew what was coming—in fact, had you asked me at the time, I would have told you my chances of survival looked pretty bleak. But then we never know what the future has in store for us, do we? How could anyone have foreseen that the admirable goal JB had worked so hard to achieve would turn out to be *my* ticket back into the driver's seat? But then I don't believe that JB or anyone else for that matter (including the sanctimonious Super E) had ever truly believed JB's star would rise as high as it did. Or that the soaring star would come with such a hefty price tag . . . not to mention loads of excess baggage.

Only *I* had foreseen that.

I just hadn't understood what it could *do* for me. Not until the first cracks began to appear in the golden façade. And by then I knew it would only be a matter of time.

And so I bided my time and waited for the moment to present itself.

And in time, it did. On that comfortable, breezy night when JB lay on the futon beside the infinity pool, gazing up at the stars, with so much conflict and confusion swimming in the troubled waters of his eyes.

That was when I knew my time had come—when the surrounding mania had reached a fever pitch and begun to close in on him, like a tremendous cacophony exploding inside his head.

You might even say the sound of that madness was my cue to step out of the shadows and take my rightful place in the spotlight.

I should take a moment here to explain something.

It may still be a little hard for you to grasp the concept of how an entity like me, who exists solely inside a person's mind, can do the things that I do—how it's possible for the *id* to take control of a body and live the life it deems best for the host. For the answer, you need only look inside yourselves, for in each and every one of you there lives and breathes an *id, ego,* and *superego.* Think back to all those moments that you've buried in your subconscious—you know, all those little indiscretions, trespasses, and lapses of morality you'd rather forget. Like the time you saw something in a shop that you didn't have enough money to purchase, but your desire was so strong you just couldn't resist taking it. Or the time you looked over at that smart kid's desk to copy the answers on his test. Or the time you lied to one or both of your parentals to avoid punishment. Or the time you turned your back on a friend because you got a better offer. Or the time you "experimented" with drugs or alcohol and got behind the wheel of a car. Or the time you lashed out in a burst of anger—by shoving someone, or shouting obscenities, or spitting . . . or even by egging a house (guilty as charged ;-)

Think back on any of those times and remember the look in your eyes while you were committing those acts—that image you see staring back at you from the mirror of your memory is the indomitable *id* (which, FYI, is *not* pronounced "I.D."—it's just plain old "id," the same way you would pronounce "it," only with a "D" instead of a "T" at the end). And everyone's *id* is the same (*I* just happen to have the extreme good fortune of being *JB's id*).

The *id* wants what it wants when it wants it, and nothing can get in its way—save for the well-developed *superego* that possesses enough strength to overpower your base desires, that is. And even then, the wily old *id* still gets his shots in every now and again . . . especially when the "soil of the soul" is particularly fertile with strife. And in the case of JB, the soil was deeply enriched by a whirlwind of success and an abundance of excess all around, which, despite the inarguable strength gifted to him by his "Wonder Twins" melding with good old Super E, allowed me to creep back in with relative ease.

Anyway, back to my story—we're getting to the good part now.

My arrival on that particular night came shortly after midnight—when JB's simmering desperation had finally reached the boiling point, and the proverbial kettle was about to start whistling its shrill scream. Timing is everything when you're dealing with JB.

I rose from the shimmering surface of the infinity pool like a specter, perfectly dry and dressed to kill in my Invisible Bully hoodie and G-Star Raw Blade Slim jeans (I love making a dramatic entrance). Though it was difficult to be certain through the fog of teen angst that shrouded him, JB looked pleased to see me. Or maybe it was just relief that I saw washing over his angelic countenance. Sometimes it's hard to tell what he's feeling at any given moment, and this particular moment was no exception.

Normally, I would have joined him on the futon, and the two of us would have stared up at the sky while reminiscing about the old days when we were little kids. But we weren't little kids anymore. We were eighteen (at least *physically*, we were—though according to Freud's Structural Model of the Psyche, I still had a three-year head start on him, which is probably why he's always treated me as if I were the older one), and I wasn't about to give up any ground. Not on this night. The time for stargazing was over. It was now time for action.

I stood on the surface of the water—a feat that has never failed to bring a glimmer of awe to JB's eyes—and waited for him to speak. And in short order, he did.

He told me he'd been thinking about the flight to New York. He said he had a bad feeling, like the feeling that kid had in *Final Destination* (the original movie, not the crap sequels). He said he didn't want to get on the plane because he felt something was going to happen, something irreversible. He stroked the *Yeshua* tattoo on the left side of his torso—a casual gesture yet rife with implication. I stroked the surface of the water with the toe of my bare foot in a reciprocal manner but kept my expression neutral. Why bother tugging at the reins when the mule is already moving forward of its own accord?

His hand was trembling as he ran his fingers through his hair, and when he let out a staggered sigh, I assumed the tears couldn't be far behind. JB is a master at the old water-works, and much to my chagrin, even *I* have trouble staying frosty when his lips begin to tremble and that first tear falls. To witness JB crying is an almost profound experience, both heartbreaking and beautiful at once—sort of like watching a magnificent painting go up in flames: tragic to see it burn, but breathtaking to watch the fire crawl over the surface of the canvas (indeed I have personally brought him to tears on numerous occasions for my own amusement).

But he didn't cry this time. And he didn't sidestep the issue with a whiny monologue about how hard and lonely life is at the top. He just told me again that he didn't want to get on the plane in the morning.

He was thinking about making up an excuse—feigning a sudden illness was at the top of the list—when I said, "You don't need to make up an excuse, and you don't need to pretend to be sick."

He wasn't shocked by my response to his unspoken thoughts (after all, we *do* share the same brain—though my skill at navigating the complex landscape of our collective psyche is undeniably superior). He just looked at me with this hopeful glint in his eyes. For a hot second I had this overwhelming urge to unleash a bit of the old school *id* on him, give him a nasty smirk and say something snide like, "*Now* who needs who, you unmitigated little turncoat?" or "Not so easy making the 'big boy' decisions, is it?"

But instead, I kept my cool.

I stroked my toe along the surface of the water again and said casually, "There is a way we could . . . disappear . . . just for a while. A day or so. Get some alone time, away from all the bad juju . . . just until you feel more able to deal with it all. Like a vacation, y'know?"

For a second I thought I might have overplayed my hand and that he was going to retreat from me, but then I could see in his eyes that he was thinking about it—and further, that he was actually *considering* it. While I waited, I made little arcs along the surface of the water with the tip of my toe, as if I couldn't care less which side of the issue he settled on.

You've probably heard that JB has a notoriously short attention span, and this is true. You may also have heard that when confronted with things he'd rather not discuss, JB can shut down and drift off, leaving you in an uncomfortable silence for as long as it takes for him to warm up to you again. Most people find it difficult to tell whether one of his sudden silences is due to something they said or if JB has simply withdrawn into himself due to some internal trigger. Indeed there are depths of JB's consciousness that even *I* can't reach. But no matter how far he drifts, I can usually pick up on the *essence* of his feelings and navigate accordingly from there. So, as he lay back gazing at the stars in silence, I was not worried in the slightest.

He was still looking at the stars when he said, "How could we do it . . . I mean like where . . . when?"

I let him stew for a moment in my own brand of silence—which was sort of cruel, I suppose, but turnabout, after all, is fair play. Then I took a measured breath and said, "At the airport."

JB shook his head. He knew we'd be surrounded by the goon squad at the airport—his security team is always on extra high alert in crowded public places, and it would be impossible to give them the slip in one of the jam-packed terminals at LAX. I was well aware of this too, but with JB you often need to present a "worst-case scenario" before hitting him with the slightly less intimidating yet still perilous alternative plan.

I waited a moment more before saying, "Or . . . "

I let it dangle there as I listened to the throbbing beat of his heart, the slight hitch in his breath, and when I felt the muscles in his jaw tense, I knew that he was not only ready to *listen*—he was ready and willing to *agree*.

As I laid out the plan for our escape, JB remained perfectly still and silent with his eyes closed. He hadn't drifted off, and he certainly wasn't ignoring me. He was listening carefully to every word, concentrating on the goal, memorizing every detail of the plan. To him, it was like a movie in which he was a captive prince in a tower cell. And I was the rogue soldier of the evil king's guard who'd come to rescue him. And though the bars of his cell were made of gold instead of lead, and the mattress upon which he slept was woven not of burlap but fine satin and stuffed not with rough straw but the softest cotton in the kingdom, though he had every amenity and luxury that any boy could possibly wish for, he was still a prisoner, and he wanted—*needed*—to escape. (I'll spare you any further details, but suffice it to say, when JB's imagination gets going—especially in his dreams, both sleeping and waking—the drama can get a bit thick . . . and fairly amusing as well.)

The plan was actually quite simple. On the ride to the airport, JB would tell the driver to pull over so he could pick up some snacks. Then he would ask the store clerk if he could use the restroom, and once we were alone in the toilet, JB would climb out the window and take off. He just needed to make sure that the driver stopped at some hole-in-the-wall shop with a single toilet that had a window.

When I was done speaking, JB lay in quiet contemplation. The silence lasted long enough for a shaft of doubt to creep into my little corner of our collective consciousness, and suddenly I had the feeling that he might be getting cold feet. I wasn't sure if pushing him was the right idea, but the silence was really starting to get to me, so I decided to give a little nudge.

"Of course, we'd need money . . . "

"I've got money," he said.

"A lot of it," I added.

"I've got money," he repeated, a little more firmly.

"And then there's the issue of Kenny to think about." Kenny was JB's numero uno bodyguard at the time, and he would have stepped in front of a speeding freight train to shield JB from harm. Getting out of Kenny's protective sight wouldn't be an easy task.

"I can handle Kenny," JB said softly.

"He's not like the other goons," I said with a casually cautious eye. "He's smart, and he's not going to just let you out of his—"

"I said I can handle him," JB snapped. "Whose side are you on anyway, bro?"

He was sitting up and looking at me now—like an errant prince gazing defiantly at the god who'd created him and given him power. There are some gods (Zeus comes

22

to immediate mind) that would have struck him down for daring to look upon them with such open disdain. But I actually liked it when he looked at me this way. It meant that I was getting under his skin . . . and working my way down to the good parts. And also, contrary to what some may believe, I am not a delusional *id*. I am fully aware of my function in the grand scheme of things. I am not a god (though, arguably, I *am* godlike). I know that I am more dependent upon JB than he is upon me—but I also know that *JB* doesn't know this. In his more spacious corner of our collective mind, I am a towering figure to be revered . . . and on occasion, even *feared*.

The trick of the whole situation is to never let him see *my* fear. And so whenever he has one of these little moments of defiance directed *inward*, I always remain cool and composed.

I looked down at him with deeply empathetic eyes and said, "I'm on *your* side, my swaggy little bro."

For a second, his eyes looked as intense as before. Then his features softened and the ghost of a smile curled briefly at one corner of his mouth because he likes it when I say things like "swaggy little bro." I mirrored his expression on the surface of the infinity pool, and for a moment we almost seemed happy. Then JB looked down morosely and began to pick at a loose thread on the futon. It was a tentative (and, more important, *submissive*) gesture, confirming that (in this particular instance, at least) he needed me more than I needed him.

I stepped forward to show that I was willing to meet him halfway. I told him that neither of us would be able to pull off this escape plan without the other. If it was to work at all, we would have to commit to it together.

I held out my fist in a gesture of solidarity, and a quiver of excitement raced through me when I felt his knuckles touch the surface of the water in a reciprocal fist bump, sealing our pact.

THE FIRST DAY

T hings didn't go exactly as planned.

JB woke early the following morning and was showered and dressed and ready to go by the time Kenny and his security team arrived. Normally, JB would try to sweet-talk Kenny into letting him take the wheel of the huge black van to the airport (or at least tease him about driving his brand new Fisker Karma Super Car while the van followed close behind), but on this particular day he just climbed into the van without a word. No one seemed to notice that the backpack slung over his shoulder was a plain canvas no-name brand instead of one of the many designer labels he usually carries his gear in . . . or that it appeared to be packed a little fuller than usual.

JB moved straight to the back of the van, dropped his backpack on the seat beside him, and took out his phone. He already had his earphones on and the volume cranked up. With the phone out and his tunes playing, the security guys knew not to disturb him. The security detail consisted of four guys, including Kenny, who sat next to the driver but kept an eye on JB in the visor mirror. It wasn't a constant thing—just a glance into the mirror every now and then—but sometimes Kenny had this way of looking at you that could make you feel like you were under surveillance, and I was starting to worry that JB might crack under the pressure. For a hot second, I was tempted to take the reins and work the old smiling charm to ease Kenny's suspicions (if in fact he actually *had* any suspicions). But on the few occasions I'd locked eyes with Kenny before, it was as if he could see right through the veil that cloaks me from just about everyone else; it was as if he was looking straight into my soul and saying: *I know exactly who you are, my friend . . . and I will move heaven and earth to keep you from messing up this kid's life.*

On each of those occasions, I'd felt a genuinely eerie chill, and I'm not going to lie: that knowing look in Kenny's eyes (the promise that it implied) put more than a little scare into me—and I don't scare easily.

In the end, I kept to my little corner of JB's mind and trusted JB to follow the plan. It was all I could do.

We were a few miles out when JB told the driver to take the Santa Monica exit and head for the 7-Eleven. He said he was thirsty and wanted a Slurpee. The driver was a new guy—otherwise what followed would never have happened. He rolled his eyes and said it was like two miles out of the way and that we wouldn't make it to the airport in time. JB told him it was less than a mile out of the way and that we'd make it to the airport in plenty of time. When the driver pressed it further and said there were other 7-Elevens along the way, I could feel something clench inside JB. Scooter had personally hired the driver and given him explicit instructions to make sure that JB arrived at the airport on time. The driver explained this to JB and promised that he'd stop at a 7-Eleven closer to the airport if there was enough time.

By this point, the other two guys, who'd both worked security for JB before, were looking down quietly, waiting for the hammer to fall, which, in mere seconds, it did.

JB looked straight into the rearview mirror and said, "What's your name?"

The driver said, "Carl."

"Well, Carl," JB said, "let me ask you something. Who pays your salary?"

Carl said, "Scooter does."

JB said, "Uh-huh. And who do you think pays Scooter's salary?"

Carl didn't say anything.

JB said, "Kenny, would you instruct Carl here to answer my question?"

Kenny sighed.

Carl looked directly at JB in the rearview mirror and said, "I suppose you do, sir."

JB laughed with a crooked grin and said, "You suppose, huh?" Then quick as a whip, the grin disappeared. "Well, let me make it crystal clear for you, then. You *suppose* correctly. But when you *suppose* that I can *wait* to quench my *thirst* until you say so, as if I'm some seven-year-old kid on a ride to grandma's house, then you ought to get your *supposer* checked out because it ain't *supposing* right. You got that, bro? Do you *suppose* that I might have a valid point here? Do you *suppose* that I wouldn't give a second thought to kicking your ass out of *my* ride and leaving you stranded on the side of the road, holding your—"

Kenny cut in, "Take the next exit."

"Scooter said—"

I goosed JB (I couldn't help myself—the driver's smug tone was starting to grate against my last nerve) and he shot forward with gritted teeth and shouted, "Say 'Scooter' one more time, bro! Say it one more time, I double-dog dare you! Say it and I'll slap that smug look right off your face, you little punk-ass bitch!"

The security guards in the back quickly got hold of JB to keep him from getting at the driver, and Carl uttered a short, humorless laugh in disbelief. "Is this kid for real?"

"I'll show you how real I am, bro," JB shouted as he lunged

for the driver again while the security guys kept him at a safe distance. "You want real? Pull over right now and I'll show you how real I am!"

Kenny said, "All right, everybody calm down. Let's all chill."

"Tell *him* to calm down! Who the hell does he think he is, talking to me like that? Tell *him* to chill."

Kenny spoke calmly to Carl. "Take the exit. I'll deal with Scooter."

"*I'll* deal with Scooter," JB snapped. "Sending this punk-ass to drive me. Just take the exit. Do as you're told, *Carl*."

By the time the van veered onto the Santa Monica exit ramp, JB was back in his seat, but he was still pissed and muttering, "That shit ain't cool, man. You don't *ever* disrespect somebody who pays your salary like that . . . treating me like I'm some little bitch-ass punk when all I want is a cold drink. I'm *thirsty*, and this guy's acting like he's my dad and shit, bro . . . you don't do somebody like that, you don't *ever* do that. That shit don't have wings, that shit don't fly."

We reached the 7-Eleven only a few minutes later, but by then I had retreated back to my little corner of our consciousness, and JB looked considerably calmer. I'd taken a real risk nudging JB into going at the driver like that, and I needed Kenny to believe that everything was chill now.

As soon as the van came to a stop in front of the store, JB opened the side door and got out. Kenny got out too, and JB said, "Are you gonna babysit me, bro?"

Kenny just smiled and shook his head. "Nah, I'm thirsty too."

JB looked into the van and addressed the two security guys. "You guys want a Slurpee? They got every flavor you can think of here." He smiled at one of the guys and said, "I *know* what *you* want, that nasty light Cranberry Sprite piss." Then to the other guy, he said, "What about you, bro? Wild Cherry?" He chuckled. "Man, you *gotta* say Wild Cherry, my swaggy brother."

More chuckling followed, along with a few good-natured jabs, and then JB turned to Carl the driver and spoke in a genuinely friendly manner, "How 'bout you, bro?"

Carl looked at him as if he wasn't sure, and JB smiled and said, "Come on, bro, don't leave me hangin here. It's all good. We're all swaggy now. I was just playin with you, pushin buttons, bro. Ask these guys, I do that kinda shizz all the time. It don't mean nothin. We're all bros, man. Come on, give it up." He extended his fist to Carl, who still looked dubious, even though he could tell the look in JB's eyes was sincere, and JB said, "Come on, man, you can't leave a swaggy lil bro hangin here."

Carl raised his fist tentatively and bumped it with JB's. And JB nodded and said, "All right, it's all good, bro." He looked happy when he said this, but his eyes looked sad, and I could tell that what he really wanted to say to Carl the driver was *I'm sorry*.

We were inside the store getting the Slurpees when JB asked the clerk if he could use the toilet. Normally clerks at convenience stores make up excuses about the restrooms being out of order, but this clerk recognized JB and told him with a smile that it was in back. Kenny, who was pouring the Slurpees, gave JB a look, and JB smiled and said, "I'm just going to take a piss, bro. I'll call you if I fall in." He headed straight back to the restroom before Kenny could protest.

The plan went south the second he saw the toilet. It was an enclosed box with no window. There was an emergency exit nearby, but the bold lettering on its huge red handle read: ALARM WILL SOUND WHEN DOOR IS OPENED.

JB's heart sank, and for a minute, he had no idea what to do. He went into the bathroom and closed the door. He looked into the mirror above the sink, but I gave him no response—I was too busy thinking. Kenny was already suspicious, I could tell that much, and the two of us, JB and I, had only made it worse—me with the attack on Carl the driver, and JB with his over-the-top swaggy sweetness afterward. It also hadn't slipped Kenny's eye that JB had put his backpack back on before getting out of the van. If he hadn't taken it off when we first got in the van, it would have been fine, but taking it off and then putting it back on just to go into a 7-Eleven was more than enough to arouse suspicion . . . especially in someone like Kenny, who was specifically trained to be suspicious of *anything* out of the ordinary.

JB was standing at the toilet, relieving himself, when our mind began to clear enough for me to formulate a new plan. I quickly came to the conclusion that we would have to chance the emergency door. The alarm might not go off—it was an old store, and in old stores doors with alarms didn't always work when you opened them. And if the alarm *did* sound off, well, JB was skinny and fast and could easily be a couple of blocks away before Kenny even made it to the back of the store. And with the van parked out front, it would be forever before any of the other guys showed up.

It was still a risky proposition, but it was the only way out. I just had to convince JB that we could make it.

He was washing his hands when his part of our brain caught up with my latest thought, and he looked into the mirror to confirm that I was in fact serious. I thought there would be a struggle of wills or at least a tense discussion, but for once the look in JB's eyes was as determined as mine.

He wanted out, and he wanted out *now*.

He dried his hands then used the paper towel to turn the doorknob (he's very fastidious and hates touching anything sticky). The click of the lock popping loose sounded like a gunshot in his ears. His heart was racing so fast it felt as if he might swoon at any moment. The door didn't creak on its hinges, but he *imagined* it did, and this got his heart throbbing, which, in turn, sent a powerful wave rushing to his head. The sound of the blood crashing at his temples was so loud that once he was outside of the bathroom, he couldn't hear a thing.

He tried listening for the sound of Kenny's voice or the clerk's, but all he could hear was the dull thunder in his eardrums.

He turned to the emergency exit, scanning it quickly to see if there might be a wire he could cut to disable the alarm before opening the door. But there was nothing. He shot a quick glance down the short and narrow hall that led back into the store. No sign of Kenny.

He turned back to the emergency exit.

It was now or never.

With every ounce of his resolve, he stepped forward, and steeling his nerves (with more than a little help from me), he pushed the big red handle toward the door and shoved. It swung open, and for an endless second JB waited for the sound of the screaming alarm. But there was no sound at all, other than that of his wildly beating heart.

And suddenly he was outside, taking a deep breath of much-needed fresh air. And then he released a shaky little laugh, and I was laughing too. We'd done it. We'd got out. The plan had worked. And now all that was left for him to do was walk away in a stealthy swagger like everything was all good.

JB was turning from the door, ready to go, when a familiar voice said, "What's up, little bro?"

It was Kenny. Crafty Kenny. Sensing that something was up, he'd gone out the front entrance of the 7-Eleven, walked around to the back of the building, and waited near the dumpster by the curb, which offered a perfect view of the emergency exit. He didn't look angry. He looked more curious than anything, and a little bit wounded too. JB just stood there frozen, unable to respond.

Kenny said, "Are you going somewhere? I'm only asking because I noticed you took your pack into the store instead of leaving it in the van."

I gave JB a mental smack on the back of his head, but I held back from saying *I told you so, dumb-ass.*

Kenny said, "You want to talk about it?"

His gaze was intense, but there was a kindness just

33

beneath the surface, and I could see that he only wanted to know what was eating JB so that he could help.

He took a step forward, and I forced JB's feet to take a step back. Their eyes remained locked, but Kenny's expression had shifted, *softened*, and it made him look momentarily weak. Perhaps Kenny sensed this because immediately his expression shifted again, making him look more like a parent or a teacher.

Kenny said, "If you're having a moment and need a break, I understand. If you want me to go back to the van while you work it out, I will. All I ask is that you show me the respect I think I've earned. If you look me in the eye and treat me like a man, then I'll do the same for you."

He paused to let it sink in, and I could feel JB absorbing it like a poison . . . a slow-acting poison that took every ounce of my considerable resolve to expel from our system.

Kenny sighed and shook his head. He could see me working from within, but this was no time for me to be hiding in the shadowy recesses of JB's consciousness—I needed to be up front and center, regardless of the risk of exposure.

Kenny's expression softened again—but only slightly, this time—and he tried another tack. "You want to run? Go ahead. Run."

You need to understand something here. Kenny never would have said this if he believed for one second that JB would actually do it. Even with my influence nudging JB on, Kenny did not believe that JB would ever run from him, certainly not with the two of them standing face to face like this. He fully expected JB to cave under the awesome pressure of his gaze, and maybe even get teary-eyed before slumping down on the curb and waiting for Kenny to come sit beside him and put his arm around him and ask what was *really* going on. Kenny was an expert at calming JB down and getting him to open up and let it all out. For a spooky moment, even *I* believed the game was over and that we'd be back in the van and headed for the airport after a little soul-soothing big bro/little bro heart-to-heart with Kenny.

But then JB did something completely unexpected. He took Kenny's last words at face value and ran.

This must have really stunned Kenny because at first all I could hear was the sound of the wind racing by JB's ears as we flew out of the back lot and dashed across the side street like Usain Bolt taking the Gold in the 100 meter dash at the Bejing Olympics. Then I could hear Kenny shouting JB's name . . . and even louder calling to the guys in the van.

As we rounded another corner on lightning-fast legs, JB could have sworn that he heard the van's tires squealing in the parking lot of the 7-Eleven, but I knew better. I knew that by then we were long gone, and nobody was about to catch up with us.

We ran for several blocks, crisscrossing down streets to hide our trail, before JB finally slowed down and went another few blocks at a casual gait.

We caught a cab about ten blocks away from the 7-Eleven, and JB asked the driver if he could take us as far as Barstow. The plan was to switch cabs in Barstow or maybe even pick up a rental car and drive the rest of the way ourselves. But when the driver said, "Hell, I'll take ya all the way to Vegas if ya want," we ditched the plan of switching rides and got in the cab.

The driver's name was Eddie, and he had a strange accent. He said he was from Jersey, so I guess that explains it. Eddie liked to talk a lot and pretty much did it nonstop for the entire ride, but JB didn't seem to mind. He was coming down from the high of our narrow escape (and feeling the first pangs of guilt over ditching Kenny), so he just sat with his face toward the open window and let the wind rush through his hair while I did the listening.

Unlike JB, I love listening to chatty people, especially the not-so-bright ones who go on and on about all sorts of nonsense. I particularly enjoy the ones who get into conspiracy theories because when those guys get fired up, you can really mess with their heads.

Eddie didn't have any conspiracy theories, but he did have some whoppers, like the story about his sister being abducted by a Dokkaebi (which is a Korean ghost). Or the one about him and his brother outrunning an escaped tiger at the Brooklyn Zoo when they were kids. But the best was the one where he was approached by the Korean mafia, who threatened to kill his entire family unless Eddie joined their organization as an international assassin. Eddie's mother was Korean, and his dad was Irish or Polish or something, and the Korean mafia wanted Eddie to step up and take the place of his uncle Joo-Won. Apparently Uncle Joo had been one of their top assassins before he got himself killed during a failed assassination attempt on some Belgian or Lithuanian dignitary (according to Eddie, his uncle was betrayed by another top assassin in the organization—Soon-Tek—but no one was ever able to prove it and bring old Soon to justice . . . or whatever passes for justice in the Korean mafia).

Anyway, it all ended quite dramatically with a rousing shoot-out at The Lawrenceville School, which is this really swanky prep school in Jersey where Eddie used to work out with this rich friend of his who was a student there. Somehow the Korean mafia guys got wind of Eddie's threadbare connection to the school and invaded the campus. They threatened to kill one student every hour until Eddie showed up and agreed to join them. Eddie showed up all right, but he had no intention of joining them, and by the bloody battle's end, Eddie was the only one left standing (apparently someone had to live to tell the tale).

We made good time across the Mojave Desert, with Eddie sticking the pedal to the floor (despite all the signs along the way warning drivers of the Highway Patrol), and JB just chilling, with his head half out the open window and the sun on his face, and me just silently chuckling away at all of Eddie's wild stories. We had another ten to fifteen miles to go when I noticed Eddie looking at JB in the rearview mirror, but I don't think JB was aware of it. He was too absorbed in looking mournfully beautiful to notice much of anything.

Eddie said, "Anybody ever tell ya that you look like that kid?"

At first, I didn't think JB had even heard Eddie, but then he said, "What kid?"

"Ya know," Eddie said, "that kid."

"Oh, that kid," JB said listlessly.

"Yeah," Eddie said. "The one who sings all those songs on the Internet and runs around with that country singer's daughter and the rest of those Mickey Mouse Club kids. You know who I'm talkin about, he's a kid just like you. That Beaver kid. You know who I'm talkin about, right?"

"Oh, yeah," JB said softly.

But I don't think Eddie heard him, because he went on, saying, "Y'know, he sings all those songs like 'That Was Me' and 'Girlfriend's Boyfriend' and stuff like that. Not really my kind of music, but he's got a real pretty voice, y'know?"

"Yeah, right," JB said, still looking out the window as if his thoughts were miles away.

"Well, you look just like him. Anybody ever tell you that?"

"Nah. I can't sing."

"That's too bad," Eddie said, "cos ya look just like him."

"I have a throat condition. I was born without a larynx."

"That sucks. I got a brother-in-law who was born without a lung—without a *lung* if ya can believe that happy crap. He can't sing either on account of he can't take a deep enough breath, y'know?"

"I hear you," JB said distantly. "My dad was born without any lungs. They had to do a graft with his identical twin brother like five minutes after they were born."

"You're shittin me."

"Nah. The brain can only last for like six minutes without oxygen, y'know, so they had to move quickly."

"Sweet *Jesus*," Eddie said. "Did he make it?"

I almost laughed out loud, but JB just kept looking out the window as if he wasn't involved in the conversation at all. "He survived," he said, "but his brother didn't make it."

"Ah, man, that's terrible."

"Yeah, but he knew the risks. He just wanted my dad to have a chance, y'know? And lucky he did, or I wouldn't be here."

"Amen to that, brother," Eddie said, and he sighed. "Man, no lungs. And look at the crap we bitch about every day when we should consider ourselves just lucky to be alive with all of our body parts intact."

"Amen to that, brother," JB said softly as he continued to gaze out the window.

The cab pulled to a stop a short while later, and Eddie said, "Here we are, kid. Sin City."

JB paid the fare then peeled an extra five hundred dollars off his roll of cash. As he extended the generous tip, he asked if Eddie could do him a solid. He asked if Eddie could forget that he ever drove a kid who looked just like that Beaver kid from Sunny Cal to Sin City.

Eddie looked at JB for a moment (and just for a second I could have almost sworn that he could see me lurking behind JB's earnest gaze), and then he smiled and said, "Who's Beaver? Never heard of him."

JB got out of the cab and closed the door. He was about to walk away when Eddie called to him. JB leaned down to the open window, and Eddie said gently, "Look, don't go flashin that wad of yours around this place. Stay on the Strip. Don't go downtown—there's nothin but a bunch of trash down there." He opened the glovebox and took out an old business card for some auto parts shop. He wrote a phone number on the back of the card, and below that, he wrote his name in neat block letters. He handed the card to JB and said, "Stick this in your wallet. If you get into trouble, you call me and I'll come on a hot dime. Don't matter what time it is, day or night, you call me and I'll come get ya. You got that?"

JB looked at the card and nodded.

"You take care of yourself, kid."

JB nodded again.

Then Eddie was gone, and it was just JB and me standing in front of the Mandalay Bay, with the rest of the Strip stretching out to the north, like a brightly lit path to our destiny.

It was around 5:30 P.M. when we finally picked out a hotel and settled in. We chose the Aria; though my epicurean taste craved the Tower Suite with all its amenities, we settled for the less extravagant Corner Suite, which was comfortable and offered a stunning view of the night skyline. JB paid for the room with the credit card of JB Swaggy. Of course, there is no such person. It's just a nickname he'd created so he could sit in on this live fan chat one night—though, in truth, it came from a combination of his initials and my own personal nomenclature, Kid Swaggy (contrary to anything you may have heard, *I* am the one and only *original* Kid Swaggy, and don't let anybody tell you different). Anyway, shortly after he'd made up this JB Swaggy account, he started to receive all sorts of email offers, like home mortgage loans and college applications, which he deleted without thought. It wasn't until he'd received a credit card application for the fictitious Mr. Swaggy that he decided to see how far he could take the joke. When he received the card in the mail a few weeks later, he thought it was pretty hysterical and wanted to show it to friends. But that's when I stepped in. With an ever so delicate nudge, I convinced him to tuck the credit card away and keep it as our little secret. And he did tuck it away, and he never told anyone about it, which, of course, ended up being most fortuitous for both of us—having an untraceable credit card can be a real plus when you're on the run and don't want anybody catching up with you.

He unzipped his backpack and put his clothes in the dressing cabinet. He'd packed two long-sleeved and three short-sleeved T-shirts, along with two pairs of jeans, six pairs of socks, six pairs of boxers, an extra hoodie, and an extra pair of sneakers. He didn't pack any shampoo or conditioner because he likes the kind they have in hotels. But he brought his own toothbrush and toothpaste and went to brush his teeth first thing after unpacking. Then he took an extended shower to get the stink of the long cab ride through the hot desert off of him, and as the warm water pelted his shoulders and sluiced down the curve of his back, he closed his eyes and let me do the thinking. For his part, he was just glad to be alone—truly alone, with no security detail waiting to escort him someplace, no handlers, no hairdressers, no makeup artist, no events coordinator, no voice trainer forcing him to run scales to keep his vocal cords limber, and no horde of screaming fans to be held at bay. No one. Just JB on his own, alone and at peace, for the first time in years. And it felt so good—so *liberating*—that all he could do was relax and let the soothing sensation of the warm running water take him away while I worked out the details of our next move.

It was a little after 7:00 P.M. when JB finally got dressed and ready to leave the room. He'd been lying on the bed in the plush Aria bathrobe for nearly an hour. Not sleeping. Just lying there with his head turned to one side as he gazed at the stunning lights on display outside the window. It wasn't until his stomach began to rumble that he realized all he'd had to eat the entire day was a couple of slices of toast before Kenny and the security team had come to pick him up. So it was out of necessity that he got up, got dressed, and headed down to the lobby.

He would have preferred to take the stairs because he gets uncomfortable in enclosed spaces, on account of this one time his cousin locked him in a toy box while they were playing hide and seek. He was only seven at the time, but he never got over it. Of course, I wasn't about to take the stairs, and since I was now the one calling the shots (at least for the most part), he got into the elevator without much resistance. It's always been interesting (as well as amusing) to watch through JB's eyes as the floor numbers flash by on the lighted panel above the doors, and I confess that I usually enjoy tweaking his anxiety levels a bit whenever we're in an elevator. But on this particular occasion, I used my considerable influence to *calm* his nerves instead because, in order for this first little solo trip through the big scary garden of the outside world to bear any edible fruit, I needed him to loosen up and relax.

We sat down at a table in Blossom, this dimly lit Chinese restaurant tucked in a corner away from the casino. The food was good, and the shadowy atmosphere was perfect for someone who didn't want to be recognized. I tried to explain to JB that even if someone *did* recognize him, they would never really *believe* it was him. After all, what would a world-famous teen pop star be doing in Vegas all by himself? I assured him that with a small amount of deception we would be able to convince just about anyone that he was merely a kid who *looked* like JB. Even Eddie the cab driver hadn't realized that his fare from Sunny Cal to Sin City was in fact "that Beaver kid"—he'd noticed the resemblance, sure, but he never would have believed that JB was the genuine article. And why would he? Why would anybody? Especially when they know that the real JB would never be allowed to set foot in the real world without at least *one* bodyguard at his side. The idea of him traveling solo would be preposterous.

I told JB all of this, but still he was worried—and when JB gets to worrying, you've got your work cut out for you.

I was actually in the process of working on it when I

noticed these two girls sitting a few tables away from us. A redhead and a brunette. They were looking in our direction and smiling like schoolgirls, but since both had drinks with little umbrellas in them, it was a safe bet that they didn't fall into the average age range of JB's fans. But then he *was* eighteen now, and so it wasn't that much of a surprise to see a couple of girls in their early twenties giving him the eye. And they *were* in fact doing just that.

And JB was aware of it, though he tried to pretend he hadn't noticed anything.

I said, "They're looking at you."

He smiled bashfully, which was sweet—and a little surprising, too, because you'd think that by this point in his career he'd be used to the attention. But he just looked down at his plate and said, "I think they're looking at you."

"Me?" I said with a grin. Then after a moment's consideration, I said, "They're looking at you, but they're seeing me *in* you . . . and it's exciting them. Chicks love dangerous guys."

JB shook his head and said, "I'm not dangerous."

I turned his gaze to the girls and said, "I am."

He must have sensed what I was about to do because his eyes got wide and he shook his head. "Don't," he said. "They'll know it's me."

"Relax," I said. "They just think you're a guy who *looks* like you. Remember what I said before: They know you'd be surrounded by a brigade of bodyguards if it really *was* you."

"But it *is* me . . . I *am* me."

"Only if you say so. To them, you're just a guy who looks like the guy . . . and the way you *look* is all that matters when you're looking."

I focused my gaze through JB's eyes and waved to the girls, and they giggled. The redhead was sipping her drink and smiling so deeply that her cheeks almost matched her hair. She had a killer body and deep green eyes that went on forever. Her friend, the brunette, had caramel-colored eyes and a healthy tan and sort of looked like Pocahontas from that animated movie—a real spitfire in disguise, who, unlike the redhead, valued her brains over her looks. You could tell at a glance that JB was smitten by her. But that was a bridge too far, and I knew it. If the kid was going to get any action, the safe money was on the redhead with the killer bod.

They joined us at our table, and JB stood like a proper gentleman until they'd taken their seats (it was a sweet move that impressed the girls, and one that I freely admit I never would have thought of—but then I've never been accused of being much of a gentleman). For the most part, I had control of JB's eyes and mouth—but JB still had a stranglehold on the tongue, and so I let the girls do the talking while I worked the old "soulful eyes and bashful smile" routine.

The girls didn't bring up the resemblance right off, but I could tell by the look in the redhead's eyes that she was debating whether or not to pop the question (and by that I don't mean she was gearing up to propose a quickie Vegas wedding with yours truly). You could tell by the glint in her clever eyes that she was leaning toward the idea that they were sitting at a table with a bona fide celebrity—but at the same time, it was clear that it wouldn't matter if JB was the genuine article or not; she was interested in him either way.

The brunette was more reserved and looked nearly as shy as JB, which only made JB tighten his grip on our tongue all the more . . . which, in turn, made it impossible for me to unleash the silvery verbiage that would make this a night to remember. I tried to speak a few times (just to give them a little more than the monosyllabic responses he was allowing us to make), but the more I pushed against JB, the tighter his grip on our tongue and vocal cords became. So I went deep and said: *If you don't relax and let me speak, they're going to think that you're hiding something . . . the redhead already has her suspicions. Just breathe and let me handle this.*

It took a moment before I could feel him easing up—and

just in the nick of time too because the waiter had returned with the check and our credit card on a tray. JB moved the card aside so he could sign the check and write in the tip.

While he was doing this, the redhead looked at the credit card and said, "Is that really your name?"

JB smiled (with a little help from me) and said, "It's actually my dad's card."

The redhead said, "What's the JB stand for?"

With me back in control, JB's response came out smoothly. "Jon Barrington. I have the same initials, only I'm Jacob Benedict, but everyone just calls both of us JB . . . which gets a little confusing at family gatherings because I've got two uncles and two cousins who also go by JB—James Bryant, Jeffrey Bryce, Jared Bruce, and Jasper Bentley."

The redhead laughed delightedly, and I gave her the old killer smile, but she still looked a little dubious.

"And no kidding, your last name really is Swaggy?"

JB said, "I hope so. Otherwise this place is gonna be shit out of luck when they process my card—" He grinned and corrected himself. "—my dad's card."

The redhead grinned too. "Is your dad like rich or something?"

"Obscenely rich," JB said.

"What does he do?"

"He's a Swiss banker," JB replied, a little surprised at how quickly I could put the words into his mouth, not to mention how smoothly I could make them roll off his tongue—it had been a long while since the last time he'd ceded this much control to me.

"So, you're Swiss," the redhead said as if she had already guessed as much. Then she added, "But you don't have an accent."

"I went to school here in the States."

"Where?" she asked, raising a clever brow; she was beginning to enjoy the game of grilling JB, and I was enjoying it too.

"The Lawrenceville School in New Jersey," JB said. "You

ever heard of it? They had a big shoot-out there way back when with the Korean mafia."

"Yeah," the redhead said, "I think I read something about that. You weren't there, were you?"

JB shook his head. "Nah, it was before my time. But I met a guy who survived it."

"Holy shit! You're kidding."

"Nah, I'm totally serious. He comes to our school once a year to give a motivational speech to the entire student body. They've got a plaque with his picture on it in the main gym where the shoot-out took place. He's a pretty cool guy."

The redhead was impressed, but the brunette just smiled politely, and I'm not going to lie: she was starting to get under my skin. Not in a bad way, but in the same way she'd gotten under JB's skin. She was starting to appeal to me as a *challenge*. And I've never been much good at resisting *any* challenge . . . especially one posed by a pretty girl.

It got even harder to resist when the brunette suddenly spoke in French to the redhead. That's when I knew the challenge would be worth pursuing because it was clear that she was only speaking in French to see if she could shoot down JB's bullshit story about being the son of a Swiss Banker.

What she said in French was, "He's only teasing you. That story is from some old movie."

It may have only been a trick of the light, but when JB smiled at her, I was pretty sure she caught a glimpse of me behind his eyes, and the spark she worked so hard at concealing within her own eyes appeared to intensify briefly.

I gave JB a nudge and he responded to her in French, "What is art but a pale imitation of life."

The line of her mouth tightened, but that spark in her eyes remained . . . smoldering at first then crackling into a small flame, and I grinned.

The redhead raised her glass and chuckled, "*Très bien, monsieur! Touché!*"

§

The redhead's name was Krystal, and the brunette's was Diana. We met up with a group of their friends in the casino, and the first words out of Krystal's mouth were, "Don't get excited. He's not who you think he is."

She introduced him as Jake but told them to just call him JB. I was mildly surprised that there were guys in the group (like JB, I'd assumed that Krystal and Diana were on an all-girls Vegas trip), but everyone was friendly, and it made JB feel less awkward, not being the only guy at the party. Even though Krystal had explained that he was just a guy who happened to look like *the* guy, some of her friends found it difficult to keep from sneaking occasional glances at him with the sort of awe that is usually reserved for genuine celebrities. Oddly, JB was okay with this. To a degree, he even enjoyed the attention and was mildly amused by the idea of a group of people enamored with his striking resemblance to himself. But mostly it just felt good to be out with people who thought he was an average guy.

They played craps while JB watched, and even though he didn't understand everything that was going on, the game was exciting and everyone seemed to be having a good time. At one point during a long roll, Krystal turned to JB and asked him to blow on the dice for luck. When he looked into her eyes after, I could see the passion there, and I knew that if he extended the invitation, Krystal would come up to our room. But as desirable as Krystal was with her smoldering eyes and swagalicious bod, JB's deeper thoughts were still on Diana. And so were mine, and both of us kept sneaking glances at her the entire time we were at the table.

When the dice JB had blown on for luck hit the table with a very lucky number, everyone cheered again because it was a huge win. Krystal was so ecstatic that she threw her arms around JB and planted a kiss on his lips that lasted long enough to draw some deep-throated "oohs" and "ahhs" as well as cheers and applause from her friends . . . all but Diana, who didn't even crack a smile.

After Krystal's run at the craps table ended, they went for drinks to celebrate. The only two who didn't drink were Diana and JB. I would have nudged him into it, but with Diana abstaining, I figured a buzzed JB wouldn't stand much of a chance, even with my surreptitious influence. For some reason, I was getting the distinct vibe that Diana was onto me, that she was aware of my presence inside JB—and further, that she didn't trust me (smart girl). So, in the end, I decided to pull back a little and let JB make the move.

It happened on the terrace outside the bar. Diana was standing at the rail, her dark hair lifting in the gentle breeze. JB came from the bar with two glasses and offered one to Diana, but all she said was, "I thought you were too young to drink."

"I am," said JB. "It's just club soda with lime." He sipped some as if to show her that it was harmless. "But if you'd like something else, I can go get it for you."

"With Daddy's money?" she asked. It didn't come off snarky, though—at least not like she was making fun of him for being the son of a rich Swiss banker. It was more of a surreptitious jab, as if to say his bogus background story hadn't fooled her for a second.

JB dropped his eyes demurely as if he were in the presence of a princess. Diana sighed and accepted the drink. She thanked him, but when she took a small sip, her eyes got wide and she let out a short laugh.

"You weren't kidding," she said with a curious expression. "There isn't anything in this."

JB said, "There's lime in it. Just a hint, but you can still taste it."

Diana gave an awkward nod and smiled in spite of herself.

JB smiled too and said, "It's good, huh?"

Diana nodded again, still smiling that somewhat bewildered yet intoxicating smile, and said, "Yeah, it's really good."

They stood there at the rail for a moment, looking out at the night sky. I could feel JB's heart beating a little faster, and I couldn't help wondering if Diana's heart was doing the same. It was hard to tell; she was a cagey girl with an exceptional poker face.

She was dressed in a light blouse that wasn't suited for the desert after dark, and when she shivered, my first instinct was to put JB's arm around her or at least take her hand. But JB made his move before I could make mine. He unzipped his hoodie, took it off, and draped it around her shoulders. She was a petite girl, and even though JB is hardly what you'd call a big guy, his hoodie looked extra large on her. The moment was so perfect that I couldn't resist nudging him to make contact, and without hesitation, he slipped his hand beneath the collar of the jacket and gently brought out her hair to drape over the hood. It was a sweet and gentle gesture that sent a subtle thrill racing throughout our body, and I was pretty sure that Diana had felt something too because when JB gently brushed the knuckles of his right hand along her cheek, she didn't pull back. And when he leaned in to kiss her lips, she let him. It was a very sweet and innocent kiss, but you could tell just how easily it could lead to something more.

JB's eyes were closed and his nose was still touching hers when she said, "Tell me something real."

Time stood still for a long moment, long enough for JB to entertain an idea that I was fairly certain would destroy all that we had built here with this beautiful girl. He was gearing up to say something when I cut him off with gentle precision, using our softest voice.

"I was twelve when my mother was killed in a car accident. I never knew my father—he took off before I was born. They sent me to live in this boys home, but I started acting out a lot, so they sent me to this other place for boys with aggression issues. It was a horrible place, filled with crazy kids, and all I wanted—all I dreamed of—was getting out. They had all sorts of 'therapy techniques' to help you with your aggression problems, like this one thing they called The Box—if a kid got too out of hand, they'd stick him in The Box. One time I got into it with this kid named Jimmy Two Times—they called him that because he said everything twice. Jimmy kept putting his fingers in my mashed potatoes at lunch and nobody would stop him, so I knocked him on his ass, and they put me in The Box for like three hours. It was this really confined space, where you had to sit with your knees pulled up to your chest and you couldn't move an inch, so by the time they let me out, I was like half crazy, and afterwards, I freaked out whenever I was in any confined space—to this day, I can't even get on an elevator without breaking a sweat.

"Anyway, I lived in that place for about two years when this guy shows up in this long black limousine and tells them that he's my dad. I don't know if he's my dad or not, but he sort of looks like me—an older version of me—and he's got a lot of money, so I figure wherever he's gonna take me, it has to be better than this madhouse, right? So I go with him, and he takes me to this really huge mansion and introduces me to his wife and tells me that she's my *real* mom. He says that the lady who raised me and got killed in the car accident was their maid and that she took me from my crib one night and disappeared, and that he and my real mom had been searching for me all these years."

I held Diana with my earnest gaze while JB let out a shaky laugh and said, "Pretty trippy story, huh?"

Diana nodded, and for a second it was hard to tell what she was thinking. Then she said, "You want me to tell you the truth?"

JB wasn't sure he wanted to hear the truth—not after the wild story I'd just laid on her—but with the color rising magnificently in her cheeks, I was spellbound. In all honesty, my curiosity over what she had to say was the only thing holding me back from taking her into JB's arms and kissing her again right then and there. The feeling was so strong that I could actually see the two of us locked in that kiss while I used JB's fingertips to caress those flaming cheeks and touch that soft, shiny hair. I wanted that so badly that I would have gladly sacrificed anything—even if it meant the two of us catching fire and burning to an ashy pile of smoldering cinders right there on the terrace, I would have done it.

But I had to hear her "truth" first. If it meant getting her up to our room, where we could get down to doing the things I was imagining, I was all ears, even if JB wasn't.

I looked at her through JB's eyes and said, "Yeah, go for it." I was smiling a smooth swaggy smile when I said this, and it made the fire inside her really burn, and *that* sent me over the moon. She shook her head. I gave her the old cool side-glance while chewing at one corner of JB's mouth (if you've seen some of those shots of JB dressed in the orange jumper in court, you know the look I'm talking about). Then I said, "Go on, mamacita, I'm listening."

I added a little nostril flare, just for good measure. This usually drives girls wild, but on that particular night it had a strange effect. Diana's expression went completely blank for a second. And then she did something totally unexpected. She told the truth.

She said she would like nothing more than to go up to JB's room and have sex with him. She said she would like nothing more than to lay there in his arms after. She said she would like nothing more than to wake up in his arms the next day and have him make love to her all over again.

JB's heart was hammering and I was ready to move in when she put a preemptive hand on our chest and said there was only one problem.

"What's that?" I'm not sure if it was me or JB who asked this, but it didn't matter.

She said, "All of those reasons are physical. You're a really good-looking guy, and I find you very attractive, but I don't know the first thing about you. Other than all of the lies you've been telling, which I suppose makes one thing clear— that you're not a very good liar. But beyond that, I still don't know anything about you, and I don't go to bed with guys that I don't know."

I responded before JB could stop me. "So, what, if I'd been straight up with you—or told you some *believable* lie—you're saying you would have slept with me then? You think it's possible for two people to meet and know each other in a few hours? Know each other well enough to have sex? In a few hours?" I snorted a humorless laugh. "Now who's lying to who?"

She shook her head and let out her own humorless laugh. "Are you for real?"

My turn. Same laugh, but with a little ironic humor this time. "That's the second time I've heard that question today."

"Maybe that's something you should think about then."

She took off JB's hoodie and tossed it to him. She was headed for the door when I called out, "That's real mature. Just walk away. That'll solve all your problems."

She turned around fast and said, "*You're* going to talk to *me* about what's mature? Now *that's* rich."

Everything went quiet for a second and then she started for the door again. I was about to say something more when JB cut me off and called out, "Wait."

It was the sound of *his* voice that stopped her this time, and when she turned, it was *him* looking back at her, and her expression shifted dramatically.

"Do you really want to hear the truth?" he said.

Diana crossed her arms over her chest and waited.

It took a second for JB to gather his nerve, and then he sighed and let it all out. The whole unvarnished truth. He told her exactly who he was and just how he came to be here— starting with the plan we'd hatched by the infinity pool the night before and going all the way up to his arrival in Vegas earlier that afternoon. He told her all of it, including his escape from the security guys at the 7-Eleven and the cab ride with Eddie and his wild tales of the Korean mafia. He just laid it all out there without omitting or embellishing upon a single detail. It was the most honest he'd ever been with someone he barely knew, and it made him feel naked and vulnerable. And as he stood there waiting for her response, I felt for him in a way that I would not have thought possible before that very moment. I knew that he was a better person than I could ever hope to be, and suddenly all I wanted was to protect him from what was coming next.

Diana laughed at him. Not a titter or giggle, but a real laugh, like she'd just heard the funniest joke. And suddenly it was JB's cheeks that were burning, and his nostrils were flaring for real this time.

Then Diana's laughter trailed off into a sigh and her expression became sad.

"I'll give you this much," she said. "That was a far better delivery than the other crap . . . almost convincing . . . you should definitely stick with that voice when you're running a line on the next girl." She paused and then added, "But be careful, you might just break her heart."

She turned and went back inside, leaving JB standing there in the chilly night alone and exposed.

It was half past one when we got back up to the room, and JB kicked off his shoes and headed straight for the bed without even turning on the lights. It had been a long day and he was exhausted. There have been times—particularly after concerts—when he's been so exhausted that he can't even get to sleep. He just lies there in bed, his body still coursing with the remnants of adrenalin from his performance, his consciousness unable (or unwilling) to cede control over to his subconscious—unable to *trust* that when he wakes, his subconscious will relinquish the temporary power it was granted the night before. This has always been one of the most frightening challenges for JB, akin to the terrifying notion of escaping a nightmare only to discover that you haven't woken at all but have merely entered another dream that is twice as terrifying as the one before it.

There are those who believe that medication is the solution (and I'm not about to deny my own attraction toward the blissful gift of certain mind-soothing substances), but on this particular night I knew what JB needed—and it wasn't the prepackaged and cunningly marketed illusion that comes in a bottle with a neat little scrip label, all tidy and legal.

What JB needed this time was a little illusion that only *I* could provide. So as he lay in the darkness of our swanky corner suite, I curled up close inside and wrapped myself around his consciousness like a warm blanket.

He didn't resist me; he rarely ever does in moments of distress when no one else is around to soothe away the pain. And I did not play the "I told you so" card. Diana's rejection of his completely sincere outpouring was enough of a slap in the face, and I saw no reason to add insult to injury. He'd learned his lesson and wasn't about to go trusting strangers again. Not anytime soon, anyway.

I closed his eyes gently and beckoned him with a facile gesture (when you exist solely inside someone's consciousness, pretty much everything you do is facile—or at least appears to be). He took my hand and together we drifted toward the nearest recesses of his mind, where dreams are born and played out like fragmented movies on screens as large as the universe itself.

In this particular dream we were floating through a sea of feminine hands, all scented with intoxicating perfume and reaching out to touch and caress him with loving grace. Sweet angel whispers accompanied our journey and spoke to him with affection, desire, anticipation, and love. Always love. Soft manicured fingers, delicate yet strong, stroking his cheeks, running through his hair. Divine sensations, lifting him higher on a bed of satin clouds, like a prince in ascension, toward that shining light at the top . . .

Of course, it was only a dream, but I knew that JB would believe it for as long as it lasted.

And as I released him into the all-encompassing feminine embrace of the angels, I drifted back to my little corner of our mind to work on the next phase of our journey.

THE SECOND DAY

We woke early the following day (when you're in Vegas it's almost impossible to sleep in, no matter how late you get to bed), and though JB was showered and dressed by 8:45 A.M., his stomach was already growling. Before we headed down to the cafe, JB hung the "do not disturb" marker on the doorknob—he was still a little nervous about being recognized and didn't want anyone, including the maid service, poking around the room while we were out.

JB took a seat at a small corner table in the cafe and ordered a waffle and a tall glass of OJ. The dining area was very bright, with loads of glass ornamentation that reflected the rays of sunlight spilling through the tall and wide wall of windows, and JB wished he'd had the foresight to grab his sunglasses before leaving the room. He would have liked to go get them, but the food came quickly, and he was starving, so he just kept his head down and concentrated on his meal. He cleaned his plate in record time and then ordered another waffle—it felt like he hadn't eaten in weeks, even though he'd had a pretty big meal the night before at Blossom, so when the waitress came with the second waffle, he dug right in.

He'd already polished off half of the new waffle when he

noticed this older woman sitting at a nearby table. She'd been watching him with this small smile on her face. At first, he wondered if he'd been eating so fast that it made him look like a pig, or if maybe he'd been chewing with his mouth open (which would have also made him look like a pig). But then the woman's smile deepened, which in turn made JB blush (older women have always been able to get him to blush, usually with nothing more than a smile). He could tell that she wasn't disgusted by his manner of eating; in fact, she looked pleased. She had the same expression his mom often gets while watching him eat a hearty meal. He guessed that it pleased most moms to see a skinny kid with a healthy appetite.

It wasn't until he'd cleaned his second plate and finished the rest of his orange juice that the woman got up and came over to his table. This threw him because he'd assumed that she would just pass by on her way out, but when she stopped in front of him, he moved to stand up.

"No, no, don't get up, dear," she said with another smile that brought a fresh crimson bloom to his cheeks. "I just wanted to say hello and give you my card."

She took a card from her bag and handed it to him. It was tasteful and expensive-looking. Ivory with embossed print, and a logo that he recognized at once because it was from one of the biggest agencies in the country. Scooter was friends with several of the agents there.

"I'm Mali," the lady said, extending her hand. "And you are?"

"Jake," JB said, figuring it would be best to stick with the same phony name he'd given the girls the night before.

"Well, it's nice to meet you, Jake," Mali said. "I'm a casting director for feature films, and there's a project in development that I'd like to have you read for. Have you ever done any performing?"

JB froze. I nudged him. He shook his head. "No, ma'am." I nudged him again. "Well, I did a few videos that I put online . . . "

Mali smiled and said, "You don't have to worry about any prior experience. I've discovered a lot of newcomers with no acting experience at all."

JB pushed a small smile and relaxed a bit.

Mali said, "I'm sure I'm not the first one to tell you this, but you bear a striking resemblance to a very famous person. Have you heard that before?"

JB worked hard to conceal his trepidation as he forced himself to nod.

Mali told him that the film she wanted him to read for was a "biopic" about an actor named River Phoenix, who'd passed away before JB was even born. From his quizzical expression, Mali could tell that he didn't know who she was talking about.

"Trust me," she said with a clever smile that reminded JB of his mom, "you look a lot like him."

Mali explained that River Phoenix was an amazingly gifted actor who had died young but left behind an exceptional body of work. She mentioned several movies—*My Own Private Idaho, The Mosquito Coast, Stand By Me, Running on Empty* (for which he'd received an Oscar nomination, she said)—but JB hadn't seen any of them.

When Mali gave him that clever "mom smile" again and said that River Phoenix *also* happened to have appeared in a little movie called *Indiana Jones and the Last Crusade*, JB's eyes instantly lit up; he definitely knew *that* movie. When she told him that it was River Phoenix who had played the younger Indiana Jones in the action-packed opening sequence, JB nodded; he remembered that sequence well. He'd actually worn out the first ten minutes of his dad's old VHS copy of *The Last Crusade* by playing the opening sequence over and over again, and for a time, his favorite catchphrase was the classic line, "That belongs in a museum!" As a kid, JB used to love popping out of nowhere and pointing his finger at people while exclaiming that line (one time he did this to his mom when she was opening a bottle of aspirin, and it gave her such a jolt that the pills went flying everywhere—she didn't get angry with him, but he felt so bad about scaring her that he never did it again).

Mali laughed a really sweet and natural laugh that made JB feel less anxious. But still, he felt guilty for deceiving her, even though she had no idea who he really was. Mali read his slightly strained expression as more of a shy kid's reaction to a surprising proposal from a complete stranger and said, "Are you here with your parents?"

"Just my dad," JB said, sticking with the details of the original lie so as not to get his story mixed up.

Mali nodded like that was good and told him to give her card to his dad and have him call her on Monday. JB was relieved to hear her add that she was headed for the airport to catch an afternoon flight to New York—the idea of running into her again while we were here in Vegas scared him because he wasn't sure if he'd be able to keep his story straight, not under the pressure of her earnest eyes. For some reason, he didn't like lying to her. He supposed it was because she reminded him of his mother, which made perfect sense because his mother has always been the one person in his life that he has never been able to lie to . . . at least not with any success.

Mali told him that it had been a pleasure to meet him and that she looked forward to hearing from him and his dad. He nodded politely in response, and as he watched her leave, something deep within began to stir.

We left the cafe at about half past nine and went for a walk on the Strip. It looked very different by the light of day, as if the mystique and majesty of the place had gone to sleep and wouldn't wake until the sun went down and the dark skyline was lit once again by the neon gods.

JB walked aimlessly for a while, so deeply adrift in his own thoughts that he was scarcely aware of any external stimuli at all—including the occasional glances he drew from passersby who could have almost sworn they'd just seen a famous person on the Vegas Strip. I knew that he was still thinking about the casting director and her tantalizing offer to come in and audition for the lead role in the River Phoenix biopic—and I knew that JB thinking about something like *that* was not good. I needed a distraction, and I found one up ahead at The Venetian: Madame Tussauds Wax Attraction.

JB had visited Madame T's in London and New York for publicity shoots with his own wax figures, but this was his first time in Vegas. In fact, he hadn't even known there was a Madame T's here until the very moment he'd stopped in front of it. For a second he looked like he had no idea how he got here, but then with a little nudge from me, he opened the door and stepped inside.

It was refreshingly cool with ambient lighting that soothed his aching eyes. It felt as if he had stepped through a porthole in time and been transported to another world where eras long past and recent had gathered in tableaux. Where Elvis Presley and John Lennon kept company with Benjamin Franklin and Albert Einstein, where the Amazing X-Men stood side by side with members of the Justice League, where world leaders once hell-bent on one another's destruction now congregated in civil accord, and where an eerily soothing silence prevailed above all else.

JB made his way through the gallery as if beckoned by some preternatural force, an ethereal whisper that only he could hear. When he reached the far end of the gallery, past all the politicians and superheroes, he stopped dead in his tracks and drew a short startled breath. Though he had worked closely with the artists in the creation of his wax sculptures and knew pretty much the entire process of building an exact likeness of himself, seeing the statue up close was always a bit jarring to him. But it was particularly jarring in the case of *this* wax figure because it didn't look quite like the others. It was him; that much was certain. But it was like an *altered* version of him.

The first thing he noticed was the most glaring: unlike the other statues, where he was dressed like a wholesome teenager, this figure was shirtless with shiny black trousers sliding off his hips to reveal his boxers. The body was hard and sinewy, with the left arm sleeved in tattoos, and the chest sported new ink art as well. Gone were the sweet boyish locks, the innocent eyes, and the hopeful expression of youth. The hair was cut close at the back and the sides of the head and swept up on top into a sleek new wave pompadour. The eyes were hard and edgy, and the mouth was curled into something that resembled a snarl.

While JB was stunned by the sight of this eerily beautiful doppelgänger standing before him, I was completely enamored. For me, it was like looking upon a god—a young Dionysus resurrected for a new age of decadence and consumption. The very notion of it thrilled me to our collective core. But JB recoiled in fear, his heart hammering wildly, his body breaking out in a cold sweat. And suddenly he felt claustrophobic, as if the walls of Madame Tussauds Wax Attraction were closing in on him.

For a spooky moment, I thought he might actually faint, and I wasn't about to let that happen. I was about to take hold of him from within and steady his shaking legs when a voice came from our left, a pleasant voice, with a soft accent that neither of us could place at first, though we both knew the speaker was female.

"He was magnificent," said the woman standing next to JB. She was an older woman, easily old enough to be JB's grandmother, and though her face displayed the lines of time, she was still very pretty. So pretty indeed that when JB turned to look at her, he was momentarily breathless.

The woman was still gazing nostalgically at the wax figure when she said, "I was at the concert in Halmstad. I went with a group of girls from the office where I worked—we were all in our late twenties, and he was scarcely past twenty-one, but we *adored* him just the same and screamed like schoolgirls when he took to the stage." She paused and then added, "Of course, I knew all the things they said about him—the drugs and the drink and the violence—but I didn't care. He made 'beautiful noise,' as they say, and his presence was *electrifying*. You could feel it in your veins. He was tragic, and he died far too young, but for that brief moment in time, he was beautiful and electrifying."

For a second JB stared at her as if she might be confused, but when he turned his attention back to the figure on display, it became instantly clear that it was *he* who'd been confused. It wasn't *his* wax sculpture at all. It was Sid Vicious, the iconic bass guitarist and vocalist of the 70s punk rock band The Sex Pistols.

JB blinked just to be certain that his eyes were not deceiving him, and the woman smiled and said, "You're too young to know about him, but your parents—or grandparents— would know. Not everybody liked him." She chuckled with that same glint of nostalgia twinkling in her lovely eyes. "He was . . . an *acquired* taste."

The woman gazed at the wax figure for a moment more and then moved on. But even after she was gone, JB still stood there, wondering how he could have ever mistaken a wax sculpture of Sid Vicious for his own. And why had he imagined all those tattoos? He only had a few tattoos himself, and the wax figure of Sid Vicious didn't have any that he could see.

As he stood there pondering this, his anxiety returned, and I took hold of that place inside him and told him to breathe, in and out, nice and deep and steady.

Relax, bro—everything's chill. Just turn around and head back in the direction we came from. One step at a time. Easy as pie, my swaggy little brother.

And then we were outside, and JB was drinking in the fresh air, and I was grinning because that's what I do when I need him to believe that everything is cool and there's no need to panic.

I got him walking back in the direction we'd come from to

clear his head and give him time to get his thoughts straight. I had intended to guide him back to the hotel, just to be on the safe side, but when he spotted this little French outdoor cafe across the street from The City Center, I knew that he wasn't ready to go inside anyplace just yet, and so we stopped to get a flavored coffee and rest for a while.

I should probably make a little confession here. There are certain things that an *id* can do . . . *if* said *id* is willing to take the time to learn what makes the rest of the brain tick—all those little nooks and crannies of the cerebrum where delicious confections such as guilt, doubt, and fear reside. For the well-versed *id*, these little receptors can provide endless hours of amusement. But, more important, they can also be used to *guide* the host along the *correct* path.

That said, I would not recommend my fellow *ids* out there start going hog wild pressing buttons inside their hosts' heads. It takes a great deal of time and practice to master the art of mental manipulation through internal stimuli—a novice *id* can inadvertently unleash a shitstorm of psychotic hubris, complete with delusions of grandeur, as evidenced by the overambitious and undisciplined *ids* of Adolf Hitler, Napoleon Bonaparte, and that creepy old Twitter queen with the mystifying duck's-ass comb-over who's constantly trolling Obama about his birth certificate, like anybody gives a crap (trust me, that super-sized Teletubby's *id* is a four-alarm dumpster fire just waiting to blow).

Of course, even an exceptionally gifted *id*, such as myself, can make a mistake and bring about the complete opposite of the desired result—which is precisely what happened when I projected the image of a futuristic JB onto that wax sculpture of Sid Vicious back at Madame T's. In the heat of the moment, it seemed like the right thing to do—a little preview of what JB and I could accomplish together. But in hindsight, I suppose it was a *bit* overzealous (everything is always so much clearer in hindsight). My little impromptu optical illusion with the wax sculpture had only succeeded in pushing JB farther away from the glorious future I had planned for the both of us.

We sat at the little table in front of the French cafe for a long time while JB quietly sipped his coffee and gazed out at the Strip. I tried to pick up on his thoughts, but when the kid shuts down, it's next to impossible to get through to him. So I just had to stay there and wait it out.

It wasn't until he'd pulled out his wallet to pay the check that his thoughts opened up to me once again. He was reaching for the JB Swaggy credit card when he saw the card that Mali the casting director had given him at breakfast—which had only been like an hour and a half ago, though it felt more like a thousand years—and as he gazed at that ivory card with the elegant print, his thoughts began to spill freely into my little corner of our consciousness like water from a brook.

He was thinking about that actor Mali had mentioned. River Phoenix. Much like JB, Phoenix had risen to the top of his profession at a very young age. But unlike JB, Phoenix hadn't been able to handle the pressure and had ultimately self-destructed—at least that's how the story was told in the articles JB had found in a quick Google search on his smartphone.

JB was still holding his phone and looking at Phoenix's picture (Mali had been right, the resemblance between Phoenix and JB was close enough that they could have easily been mistaken for brothers), and the longer he stared at that image, the more he wanted to know about Phoenix. Not Internet gossip or anything like that. He wanted to know the *real* River Phoenix—and he understood that the clearest path to that end would be through Phoenix's films. Unlike most people, who gobble up gossip and "in-depth investigative reporting" like ravenous animals in their quest to get at the soul of their favorite celebs, JB has always understood that the *true* soul of any celebrity can much more easily be accessed through his or her work—which is ironic when you think about it, considering that their work (whether it be performance, writing, or art) is the one thing that *all* celebs are not only willing but *eager* to share with the entire world.

JB left the cafe and went to the Town Square mall to purchase an iPad (he hadn't packed his own, because he hadn't foreseen the need of it—nor had I). Then he headed back to our room at the Aria to download the movies that Mali had mentioned.

We sat on the bed and watched three of the four movies back to back, which took a little over five and a half hours. It would have taken even longer, but after only a few minutes into *Stand By Me*, JB realized that he'd already seen it and shut it off. It was nothing against the movie itself—which he remembered enjoying very much the first time he'd seen it— he just wanted to get to the other movies he hadn't yet seen.

My Own Private Idaho was by far the strangest of the three; in it Phoenix played a narcoleptic hustler who only wants to be loved but ends up getting used and discarded, and the whole thing just made JB feel depressed. In *The Mosquito Coast*, Phoenix played a kid whose crazy dad uproots his family from their normal life and takes them to live in some jungle in Central America so he can build an ice machine. It wasn't as strange as the *Idaho* one, but still it was pretty depressing seeing the kid trapped in the jungle while his dad just gets loonier and loonier. After watching these two movies in a row, JB began to think, if the rest of Phoenix's films were even half as depressing, it was no wonder the guy had gone into a downward spiral in his personal life.

JB liked *Running on Empty* the best and was really glad he'd saved it for the last because even though it was about another kid trapped in a life he desperately wished to escape from, unlike the first two movies, this one had a sense of real hope. The kid's parents are radical eco-activists who blew up a napalm lab back in the 70s to protest the war and have been on the run from the FBI ever since. So they keep having to move from place to place and change their identities to avoid being arrested, and the kid Phoenix plays has had to live his entire life on the run for something he had nothing to do with.

This really struck a chord in JB. He knew that he wasn't exactly like the kid in the movie. It wasn't like someone had placed a gun to his head and forced him to do the videos that had gained him so many followers on YouTube. Nor was it like he'd been forced to take the deal to become a recording artist and go on tour. He fully understood that he'd made these decisions on his own. But still he couldn't help feeling that the decision he'd made—the decision that had irrevocably changed the course of his life and placed him under the extreme pressure that he now faced on a daily basis—should have never been *his* to make in the first place. He was just a kid, and what kid would say no to fame and fortune? What kid could possibly *conceive* of the darker realities that fame and fortune would bring with it?

He didn't want to lay blame, but he couldn't help thinking that the adults should have stepped up and made a decision in the best interests of the kid who didn't know any better. They should have *protected* him from a life on the run. And in *that* way, he felt a *lot* like the kid in *Running on Empty*.

But like I said, for this particular River Phoenix character, there was a silver lining of hope. In the end, he gets away from his life on the run with his parents and goes on to have the life he's dreamed of for so long.

This got JB thinking, and for a while he indulged in this delicious little fantasy of trading up his old life for a new one. He imagined what it would be like to become Jake Swaggy, the kid who looks just like JB the pop star. He imagined that this new life could somehow be easier because, after all, Jake Swaggy only *looked* like JB. Oh, there might be a little attention at first—particularly from JB's hardcore fan base—but then, after a while, the attention would die down because the main focus would still be on JB, the real star.

Here his imagination went into overdrive as the pieces of his fantastic fantasy fell nicely into place. He would become

Jake Swaggy on the side and build a respectable career as an actor while continuing to be JB the pop star in the forefront. Then after a time, when everyone truly believed that Jake and JB were in fact two separate people who just happened to look alike, JB the pop star would announce to his fans that he was retiring, that he'd purchased a secluded island someplace far away and planned to live out his life there, quietly and out of the public eye. And once that was done, he would devote all of his time to being Jake Swaggy.

Of course, there would still be a few things he'd need to take care of to complete his transformation. He would go to a far-off foreign country that no one has ever heard of and have the tattoos removed, so there wouldn't be any identifying marks that could tie him to his former life (in his imagination this sounded like a very workable plan because he didn't have all that many tattoos yet, and so it wouldn't be that difficult getting rid of them—he might even keep one and say that he got it to honor the memory of his retired look-alike).

The more he thought about it, the more he believed it could actually work. He *could* shed his old persona for a new one. He could recreate himself into the image that *he* desired and not go on living in the image that others had designed, packaged, and marketed. The most important thing was to get the ball rolling and contact Mali first thing on Monday morning. Everything would be fine then. He felt sure of it. He would be on his way to his own happy ending.

It was coming on 7:00 p.m. when JB realized that he'd been sitting in the room watching movies and fantasizing about his new life for over seven hours. In all that time, I had not interrupted him. I had simply held my position of observance at the periphery of his consciousness, waiting for the inevitable downswing. But by the time he'd showered and put on a fresh set of clothes (the kid is absolutely obsessed with cleanliness and personal hygiene), his little fantasy was still spinning on overdrive upstairs.

This was when I began to think a little "intervention" might be necessary. Normally his fantasies fade out as quickly as they come, but this one appeared to have some real staying power. He was actually *serious* about jettisoning the life we had worked so hard to build so he could become something as mundane as an *actor!*

Now, don't get me wrong here. I have no problem with actors, per se. In fact, I respect them for what they do, and I know that it's hard work. But let's be honest: unless you can be Jack Nicholson or Daniel Day-Lewis or Leonardo DiCaprio, what's the point? And let's face it, the odds on JB becoming the next Jack, DD-L, or Leo would be about nine hundred trillion—times infinity—to one. The best that a kid like JB could hope for in an acting career would be snagging the role in the River Phoenix biopic. And even if by some miracle he was able to pull off that role with any level of proficiency, his chances of moving on to equally challenging and rewarding roles would be bleak at best. In all likelihood, he would just end up on some hokey CW show playing a pouty-mouthed, doe-eyed vampire brimming with teen angst . . . until he hit his thirties, that is, and then it would be straight to one of those *CSI* shows (and we all know how well *that* little foray into acting worked out for him a few years back).

JB wanted to have dinner at the Aria again, but I used his newfound dream of ditching our life for an acting career to guide him to Planet Hollywood instead. I knew there wouldn't be any movie stars hanging out and having a burger (if you're looking for movie stars, the last place you'll find them is at Planet Hollywood), but I figured we stood a very good chance of running into a few *aspiring* movie stars. I figured it would be fairly easy to strike up a conversation with a few of them and that after a few hours of listening to their pretentious crap, JB would have a swift turnaround on his bright idea of trading up the real stardom we'd achieved for a ridiculous pipe dream.

It actually worked out even better than I'd thought it would. JB took a corner booth away from the crowd and kept his attention focused on his plate throughout the meal. But this didn't keep our server, a tall kid with longish copper-colored hair and pale blue eyes, from grinning at him and whispering to his coworkers at the servers' station. He wasn't mocking JB; he was simply marveling at JB's striking resemblance to a certain famous person . . . and JB was about one hundred and ten percent sure that the famous person in question was *not* the late River Phoenix.

The inevitable came when JB finished eating and the copper-topped server brought him the check. JB was going to pay with cash, but when the kid asked him if he could settle an argument, JB pulled out the credit card instead and set it on top of the bill.

The server's eyes twinkled. "I knew it," he said with a crooked grin. Then he called over his shoulder to one of the other servers, "You owe me twenty bucks, Marc. It's not him."

JB tried not to watch as his server showed the credit card to the others at the servers' station, but he could hear little bits of their conversation.

The server named Marc was saying, "That doesn't mean shit, dude. It could still be him. Lots of celebrities have fake IDs to hide their real identity."

Copper-top said, "You're just pissed because you lost the bet, dude."

Marc rolled his eyes and said, "JB Swaggy? For real? Come on, Jabona, how gullible are you?"

Copper-top laughed and said, "Riiiiight, cos if he was gonna make up a fake name, he'd *definitely* go with something like 'JB Swaggy' and hang out at Planet Hollywood with no entourage and no security, cos that's what megastars do all the time. Come on, yo, how stupid are *you*?"

That seemed to stump Marc, and he got quiet.

A third server, a guy named Cory, said, "Yeah, but you gotta admit, he *does* look like him."

Copper-top pulled the guest copy of the receipt from the register and said with a shrug, "Like they say, bro: Everybody has a double somewhere in the world." Then before heading back to the table with the credit slip for JB to sign, Copper-top turned to the one named Marc and said with a laugh, "Twenty bucks, please, bizzotch."

Copper-top, whose real name turned out to be Jonah (or as his friends called him, "Jabona"), brought JB a complimentary slice of cheesecake with the check and told him it was store policy that all celebrity look-alikes get a free dessert. He grinned when he said this, and JB couldn't help but return the gesture with a modest but genuine smile. He could tell that Jonah was a good guy, and it made him feel normal to be around somebody who had no expectations or ulterior motives. In another life, he could see himself being friends with a guy like Jonah and just doing normal things like skateboarding and playing video games and hanging out, and maybe even waiting tables at Planet Hollywood.

While JB ate the cheesecake and listened to the conversation and laughter of the three servers in the background—the normal chatter of teenage boys going on about girls and movies and the like—I could feel his dream of swapping our life for an acting career gently sliding into the graveyard of our subconscious, where countless other fleeting fancies had been laid to rest.

He still wanted out of our present life, but he no longer wanted to swap one spotlight for another.

Now he was thinking about a life away from fame altogether. Now he was thinking that what he *really* wanted was to be a normal teenager, like the three guys doing their side jobs at a big booth near the servers' station. He wanted to be laughing and chatting it up right along with them while filling salt and pepper shakers and wiping down tables with a damp bar towel.

He just wanted to be one of the guys.
He suddenly wanted that more than anything.

We were getting ready to leave when Jonah came to bus our table. JB thanked him for the cheesecake, and Jonah thanked him for the tip (an overly generous one that surely would have raised suspicion had our server been that Marc kid). JB smiled like it was no biggie. He was turning to go when Jonah extended his fist and said, "I'm Jonah, by the way."

JB responded to the fist bump and said, "Jake."

Jonah grinned his crooked grin and said, "Jake Swaggy. The other JB." He tipped a nod in the direction of his friends, who were racing to see which could get the rest of his side jobs done faster. "Don't pay any attention to those guys. They're half-baked most of the time." Then he raised a confidential brow. "I'll admit, I almost thought you were him too—for like five seconds—but then I was like, 'Nah, couldn't be.' Besides, I heard the guy is like a total dick when people recognize him in public . . . " He rolled his eyes in the general direction of his buddies and grinned. " . . . especially when it's a couple of geeky burnouts gushing like little girls. I heard that really gets him pissy."

JB laughed, a genuine laugh that made him feel genuinely good. Jonah laughed too, then shook his head and said, "Nah, they're cool. We all went to high school together . . . and now we work here . . . which should tell you something about the quality of education at our high school."

JB laughed again.

Jonah said, "So, you still in school?"

JB shook his head.

Jonah nodded like he could dig it. "That's cool. High school sucks—especially public high school. You can't learn anything until you get to college."

JB said, "Are you in college?"

"Nah. My older brother is, and he says it's way different

than high school. Teachers aren't such dicks, I guess. You in college?"

JB shook his head. "I'm taking a year off . . . to travel with my dad."

He wasn't sure why he'd added that last part, but Jonah didn't seem to find it unusual; he simply nodded and said, "Cool. So you're here with your dad?"

JB nodded, half expecting Jonah to press for more, but Jonah just nodded back like it was all good, and JB gave a silent sigh of relief. For some reason he was having as much trouble lying to Jonah as he'd had with Mali the casting director.

When Jonah said that he and the guys were getting off work in twenty and heading out to a party at a friend's place, JB figured it was his cue to go. But then Jonah surprised him by asking if he'd like to come along, and JB surprised himself by responding without thought.

"Yeah, cool."

We got to the party at half past nine. It was in the basement of this really swanky house a few miles off the Strip. Jonah had insisted that JB call his dad for permission. JB was both surprised and touched by this, but since he didn't have a dad to call, it made things a little difficult. What made it even more difficult was that Jonah stood right there at the table waiting for JB to contact his dad, so when JB didn't make a move, I did.

I took out his cell phone and scrolled through the list of contacts. I needed to find a number I could send a text to and get a response from, so that Jonah would hear the text tone and know that JB wasn't just faking it. The trouble was, all of his contacts were friends and family who wouldn't respond with just a single text—one message sent to any person on that list would lead to a slew of texts that neither JB nor I wanted to deal with just then.

I was about to give up and dial a number at random (which would have really looked suspicious—why would a kid not have his own dad's number in his contacts list?) when I came across the number of someone who definitely wouldn't send repeated texts back. The only question was, would she even respond to a single text? Since it was pretty much the only available option, I took a shot and clicked on the contact marked "Diana" (Krystal had given JB Diana's number back at Blossom while Diana was in the restroom—she'd given him her own number too but said that if he wanted to get in touch to call Diana's number instead because the battery on her own phone had died).

I typed this message in French: ARE YOU READY TO ACCEPT THE TRUTH?

It took only a few seconds for the response: WHO IS THIS?

I thought about it for a second and then typed JB's real name and added: BUT YOU'VE KNOWN THAT ALL ALONG, HAVEN'T YOU, PRINCESS. I capped this message with a winking smiley face emoji.

The response came back: HOW DID YOU GET THIS NUMBER?

I typed: I HAVE MY WAYS. YOU WANT TO MEET FOR DRINKS AND A LITTLE PILLOW TALK, AND I'LL TELL YOU ALL MY SECRETS?

Her response was immediate: GROW UP. AND DON'T SEND ME ANY MORE TEXTS.

I sent one more anyway, just to ensure that she wouldn't have a change of heart and try to contact JB later. I typed: AS LONG AS YOU LOVE ME, BABY.

That did it. I could almost see the crimson flames rising to her cheeks as she switched off her phone for the night, and I couldn't help but grin while imagining what a fiery pistol she'd be between the sheets. Of course, I kept JB's expression neutral when I turned his eyes to Jonah and said, "Yeah, it's all good. My dad says I can stay out as late as I like."

Jonah introduced JB as Jake to his friends at the party, and surprisingly they all appeared to accept it without question. A few marveled at the uncanny resemblance, but no one disputed the claim that JB wasn't the real JB—of course, this was likely due to the fact that most of them were already pretty baked by the time we'd arrived, and also that none of them looked like the type who would ever listen to any of JB's music or have even the slightest interest in him.

The basement was one of those huge walk-ins, with three sets of French doors along the wide outer wall, all of which opened onto this sprawling back lawn with an in-ground swimming pool that looked like something out of *The Great Gatsby* (JB had read that book in seventh grade English Lit— he thought it was just okay, but I was enamored with it; all that wealth and opulence only served to fuel my desire for our success). All three sets of French doors stood open, and most of the kids at the party were outside, yet still a sweet cloud of premium Jamaican Ganja permeated the huge basement. Some kid in torn blue jeans and a black T-shirt (with white print that proclaimed: I DO WHAT THE VOICES IN MY HEAD TELL ME TO) sat on an oversized beanbag chair in a corner, toking on an ornate hookah that looked like something out of *Alice in Wonderland*. When he caught JB looking at him, he hummed the refrain of one of JB's earlier hits and grinned and nodded like it was all good. JB noticed that this kid had a tattoo on the inside of his forearm, just below the crook, that read: FAITH. When the kid noticed JB looking at the tattoo, he grinned and nodded like it was still all good, and then passed out.

We had been there for about a half hour when a couple of guys started setting up microphones and speakers at one end of the basement. Jonah explained to JB that they used to set up outside, but the neighbors complained about the noise and so now they could only play inside. Jonah nodded to this one guy with short dark hair and intense hazel eyes, who was tuning an acoustic guitar (JB couldn't help noticing that it was a left-handed guitar). Jonah told JB that the guy's name was Caleb and that he was a really good guitarist and that he also played the drums. JB didn't see any drums, just a few guitars and a keyboard, so he assumed they wouldn't be playing anything too heavy, and he was right. It was pretty much all acoustic sets of classic rock, mixed in with some original compositions.

75

They did this one cover of a song called *Smiles & Glances* by some indie group from Chicago named Final Round (the original version is on Youtube—the video is only so-so, but the song rocks). It was a fast-paced, catchy tune sung from the perspective of a stalker as a sort of love letter to the object of his obsession. JB liked it, but at the same time, it made him feel a little uneasy. I thought it was the most magnificently perfect song I'd ever heard. It gave me chills and stoked a fire within. I understood that it was written from the perspective of a guy to a girl, but still it felt like the lyrics were coming directly from my soul and pointed at JB, especially this one line of the chorus that went:

> *I swear that there's no one*
> *that can come between me and you—*
> *if they tried then I'd*
> *feel sorry for them.*

The third and final time that line was sung, JB glanced at his reflection in the French doors, and from those mullioned panes of glass, I gazed back at him with a small dark smile.

They had done like three or four sets when the lead singer, a kid named Logan, took the mic and told the crowd that they had a "sort of celebrity" in their midst tonight. He grinned and confessed that it wasn't a *real* celebrity but someone who could easily pass for one. Then he told the crowd that maybe if they all worked together, they might be able to coax this "celebralike" into giving a one-time-only live performance.

The challenge set everyone off—even the ones who were too high to know what Logan was talking about—and as they all began to cheer and chant "JB, JB, JB" over and over, Jonah leaned in close and said, "Dude, I swear I had no idea this was going to happen. You don't have to do anything."

Jonah was raising his hands to quiet the crowd and tell them that Logan was only joking when (without any prompting from me, I swear it) JB stepped up to the mic. Logan leaned in close to his ear to be heard over the sound of the crowd and said, "Do you know any of his songs?"

JB shook his head and asked Logan if he knew Iron & Wine's *Trapeze Swinger*. Logan nodded with a sly smile of respect at JB's choice. When Logan turned to the guy at the keyboard to give him the selection, JB asked Caleb if he could borrow his guitar. They were set up in moments, with JB sitting on a stool in the center and Logan and the others in backup positions.

From the moment the first gentle guitar chords were struck, a tingle raced through my corner of our collective psyche, and when the soft sound of JB's voice came with the opening lyrics, I felt myself falling, as if down a long, slow drop, with no bottom in sight. Then it was like I was float-ing on a gentle breeze, being carried back to a time before time when the entire universe was simply me and JB lying under the stars on warm summer nights, both of us lost in our dreams. I couldn't help but believe that he'd chosen this song deliberately. It was the one song that could do to me what nothing else inside or outside of JB's mind could ever hope to do: Tame my innate hubris and bring me to a state of unequiv-ocal humility.

If you think I'm being overly dramatic here, go download *The Trapeze Swinger* (and by that, I mean *legally*—when an artist pours his heart and soul into a song, the theft of that song is *not* a victimless crime, so don't be a *douche,* just pay the $1.29, you cheap pricks). Listen to those nostalgic lyrics cut gently through your core, exposing every tender nerve ending to a collage of memories so beautiful they can actually elicit pain. Plug in your earphones, pump up the volume, and imagine that lovely sound coming from *inside* your head, where you can't turn away from it, and *then* come and tell Swaggy how overly dramatic you think he is.

JB was halfway through the song when I noticed this tall guy with an Obama haircut standing at the back of the crowd. He was leaning against the jam of one of the French doors in this cool way that set him apart from the rest of the kids. He had dark eyes and sharp features that made him look not older but *wiser* than his peers. And he seemed to be looking straight through JB, as if he knew something that the others at the party did not . . . as if he knew Jake Swaggy's *true* identity and was merely trying to figure out why a world-famous pop star was here in Vegas pretending to be a regular kid at a party.

His name was Nick, and after JB's performance (which drew the loudest applause of the night), Jonah introduced him to JB. Nick smiled politely when he shook hands with JB, and JB couldn't help thinking that Nick's smile made him look a little vulpine, like a fox in the chicken coop or one of those vamps on that HBO series, *True Blood*. For me it was different. I saw Nick as a stealthy panther on the hunt. Cool, calm, and patient. A vigilant force of the night, always on the lookout, and ready to pounce at a moment's notice . . . in other words, my kind of guy.

From the moment Nick arrived, it was clear that he was the alpha of the group, and so when he suggested we ditch the party and take a ride, no one stood in opposition, not even Jonah.

Eight of us took off in two separate cars—Jonah's buddies from Planet Hollywood, Cory and Marc, and another guy everybody called Toad, went with Jonah in his car, and JB road with Nick and these two guys named Mason and Giancarlo in Nick's battered Jeep (Jonah tried to get JB into his car but gave in when Nick teased, "Jesus, J-Bone, let up on the leash."). They swiped some beer from the party and drove to Mason's place, a huge old three-story house a few miles to the west of the party. JB felt a chill when he saw the sign on the front lawn that read: McPHERSON FUNERAL HOME. As Nick brought the Jeep to a stop behind Jonah's Civic, he dropped a sly wink at JB in the rearview mirror.

"Everybody has that reaction when they first come to Mace's house," he said with a grin. "Don't sweat it, Jake. It's just a job. Somebody's got to do it. Mace here'll be doing it one day, just like his old man and his gramps before him."

"Not me," Mace said with a goofy chuckle. "My little brother can have the whole thing—he likes hangin with dead people. I'm outta here as soon as I graduate."

Nick's grin deepened. "Yeah, right, like you've never thought about hookin up with a 'cold one' in your old man's basement.'"

Giancarlo shrieked with laughter. "Ah, c'mon, yo, that is just sick."

Nick said smoothly, "The heart wants what the heart wants, right, Mace?"

Mason chuckled again and said, "Yup."

I could feel JB's heart beating a little faster, and I smiled (I'm not sure why, but his fear often excites me). I knew that when we got out of the car, he was going to pull Jonah aside and tell him that he needed to go back to the Strip. He had already come up with an excuse. He would say that his dad had sent him a text, that there had been a change of plans and that they needed to catch an early flight out of Vegas in the morning, and that he had to get back to the Strip at once. He didn't care if the other guys laughed at him for knuckling under to Daddy's call. All that mattered was that he didn't want to go inside Mason's house.

But when Jonah arrived and got out of his car, something completely unexpected happened. Mason called out, "I hope you got your keys, bro, cos mine are up in my room."

Jonah rolled his eyes like it was the stupidest question ever and said, "I *drove*, dude. Of course I have my keys."

Mason laughed like Jonah's response was the funniest thing he'd ever heard and said, "My bad. I'm pretty messed up." And then he snorted laughter again.

Jonah told him to keep it down before he woke their parents. Mason said that their parents slept like the dead and then after a short, thoughtful beat, started laughing even harder. Toad, who was nearly as high as Mason, said, "Good one, bro." Nick grinned. Jonah just glared at Mason.

It wasn't until then that JB saw the family resemblance, which was actually fairly striking. Still, he couldn't help thinking that Jonah seemed more like the older brother in college and Mason seemed more like the teenager who should be working at Planet Hollywood. He was still a little apprehensive about going into a funeral home after dark, but he trusted Jonah, and now that he knew it was Jonah's house, his need to leave quietly slipped away, and he followed the rest of the guys inside.

We went to the downstairs parlor, which looked like a smoking room in one of those old movies set in England before the turn of the twentieth century, complete with ornate wood-paneled walls, rich leather furniture, plush carpeting, and a huge fireplace. The adjoining room was where they kept the display coffins.

Atop one of the closed caskets, a large black cat lay curled into a comfortable ball with one front leg poking out from under his chin. He opened his eyes and peered at us through the archway. Briefly, he flexed the claws of the outstretched paw before closing his eyes with a soft sigh.

JB loves all animals. I'm not so copacetic with them. Especially felines—they don't trust me, and the feeling is mutual. But just for a second there, I could have sworn that big brute could see me in the shadows behind JB's eyes, and it gave me a shiver.

Jonah turned on the stereo system and set the station to a classic rock channel before joining the rest of the guys in the sitting area, where Mason was rolling a fat joint. They passed the joint around, and everyone took a hit, except for JB. He passed it on to Cory, who took a deep drag and said, "You've got a really good voice, man."

"Yeah, bro," Giancarlo said, "You should be out there

doing concerts and shit—you're like *way* better than that little Beaver bitch. *You* can actually sing . . . *live*."

JB surprised himself by saying, "He sings live."

Giancarlo said, "Nah, bro, that shit's all like lip-synced. None of those pricks sing live. My cousin's a roadie, and he's seen all that shit they do to make those guys look like they're singing. It's all like shadows and smoke."

Jonah said, "You mean smoke and mirrors?"

Giancarlo said, "Shut up, bitch, 'fore I put you in one of those coffins. Yeah, that's what I mean. It's all like magic, like that Criss Angel shit, y'know?" He took a deep hit off the joint and then tapped his forehead with his thumb while looking directly into JB's eyes. "Just like the Mindfreak, bro. They make you *believe* the illusion is real. That shit happens all the time out there. But you . . . your voice is like pure and uncut. You don't need any of that Auto-Tune crap and backup tracks."

JB was looking into Giancarlo's eyes and listening intently when Giancarlo suddenly shook his head fast with a little shiver and looked away with a grin.

"Damn, bro, you're freakin me out," Giancarlo said with a nervous laugh. "You're all givin me that intense gaze shit, and lookin' just like that little punk-ass Beaver." He chuckled low. "Don't mindfreak me, bro."

Jonah said, "You *are* a mindfreak, Carlo."

The other guys laughed at this.

Giancarlo said, "What'd I tell you 'bout that shit, bro? I'll put you in one of those coffins, don't test this steel."

The laughter got louder. Even Nick, who'd been gazing like a suspicious cop at JB the entire time, cracked a grin.

Then Giancarlo put a hand on JB's shoulder and said, "Nah, I'm serious, bro. You got real talent. You should do concerts and charge like half what that little preppy bitch does and steal all his fans. You could be the New Beaver, who's not such a dick and really sings live. Am I right? You gotta believe . . . like really *believe*. That shit is real, bro." Then he retracted his hand and chuckled. "Just don't be givin the evil eye, y'know?"

The guys laughed again as Giancarlo high-fived Mason and said, "For real. Am I true, bro?" And Mason concurred that Giancarlo was indeed true.

The laughter was dying down when Nick spoke for the first time, and there was no mistaking whom he was speaking to because his eyes were fixed on JB.

"So where are you from, dude?"

JB met Nick's gaze, and at first he was thinking of giving him the same story he'd passed off on Krystal and Diana, but something told him that Nick already knew the answer to his question, and so he didn't say anything. At this point, I was personally starting to tire of both Nick's gaze and his attitude (I know what I said about him being my kind of guy, but his whole cagier-than-thou-cool-silent-staring-act was starting to wear thin, even on me), so I took hold of the old vocal cords and said, "Does it matter?"

Nick shook his head like it was all nothing. "Nah, I guess not." Then he added, casually, "Unless you've got something to hide, that is." He looked into JB's eyes again. "You don't have anything to hide, do you, Jake?"

"Nope."

Nick nodded and let out a measured breath. Then he said, "You want to know what I think?"

JB didn't say anything, and for once I followed his lead because I got the feeling that this could possibly lead to something productive . . . that maybe this smug prick with his cool gaze, Obama haircut, and laid back manner might end up providing just the sort of nudge to knock the silly notion of becoming a "regular kid" out of JB's head once and for all. Sometimes all it takes to send a wayward celeb racing back to the safety of his gated existence is a good old-fashioned encounter with one of the "regular folk"—especially one who looks upon celebs with contempt . . . and I was starting to get the distinct impression that Nick's contempt ran deeper than most.

Nick continued without any prompting. "I think you are exactly who you look like. I think you're a spoiled prince who got bored with all the glitter and decided to see how the other half lives. I think that when you finally tire of slumming it, you'll go back to your castle up on high and have a good laugh with your entourage over how easily you fooled all the lowly serfs below."

Everyone sat frozen, including JB. I had to admit, Nick's little rundown was amazingly close to the mark. I would have liked to believe that he was just fishing and got lucky, but something in his cool gaze told me different. JB was still too stunned to react—his heart was pounding so fast, I thought he was going to crack and confess everything right there.

I was getting ready to make a preemptive move—just in case—when Jonah said, "Dude, if you have a problem, you can leave."

At first JB thought Jonah was talking to him, but when he looked up, he could see that Jonah's gaze was fixed on Nick, and he got the feeling there was some tense history between the two of them.

Nick said casually, "I don't have any problem."

Mason said, "Don't be a little bitch to my friends, Jabona." And to Nick, he said, "Dude, don't even listen to him."

"No, dude," Jonah said, "*do* listen to me. This isn't your home anymore, Mace. You don't live here. I do. And if you and your friends can't respect my friends, then you can get out too."

JB was surprised to see that Jonah was serious, and even more surprised to see Mason back down.

"Jesus, bro, chill," Mason said in a low wounded mumble. "He was just messin with your boy. Tell him you're sorry, Nick. He's steppin all over my high . . . *damn*."

Nick was still gazing at JB with his cagey eyes. Then he

smiled and said, "My bad." Things looked like they were calming down when Nick added casually, "But there *is* a way to prove it . . . "

Jonah's jaw clenched, and Nick held up his hands, as if to say "no foul." JB remained silent, waiting for Nick to continue.

Nick said, "It's a well-known fact that a certain teen pop star is hyper claustrophobic . . . so, all Jake here would have to do to prove that he's *not* said teen pop star is climb into one of those caskets back there and stay inside for one minute . . . without totally losing it." He turned his gaze back to JB and said, "You could manage one minute inside a closed casket, couldn't you, Jake?"

JB's heart was pounding now, and I wrapped myself around him from within to keep him from showing any signs that Nick's little challenge was getting under his skin.

Giancarlo looked at Nick with wide eyes and uttered a low chuckle. "Damn, bro, you is one icy cold *pandillero*. You got like one of those evil genius minds that come up with that freaky torture shit. You should be like NSA or some shit. I'm serious, bro, you're like all Zero Dark Thirty, mindfreaking me out and shit."

Nick's cool gaze was still locked on JB. "Just sixty seconds inside a coffin, Jake. A small price to pay to prove that you are who you say you are . . . "

Mason chuckled. Nick's gaze teemed with sparks.

Jonah stood up and said, "Get out." He pointed at Mason. "You too."

"What the—" Mason cried. "I didn't even *do* anything, little bro."

Jonah said, "Mace, I'm dead serious. Unless you want your friends to see you get your ass kicked by your little brother, you'll take this piece of shit and get out of here right now."

Mason held up his hands and slurred, "I'm on your side, bro . . . damn . . . I didn't even . . . this is so . . . "

I forced JB's mouth to work, and the words came tumbling out before he could stop them. "I'll do it."

Giancarlo's eyes flashed with excitement. Nick's gaze remained cool. Mason slurred with a sloppy grin, *"See?* He *wants* to . . . "

"No," Jonah said bluntly.

But I already had JB's legs moving, and the rest of the guys followed him into the adjoining room where the caskets were on display. JB shot a look at Nick and for a second he thought he saw a flicker of doubt beneath the hard surface of Nick's gaze.

Then a cool grin curled at one corner of Nick's mouth. "Sixty seconds," he said smoothly. "It'll be over before you know it, right, Jake?"

JB held his gaze on Nick until Nick shifted his own gaze to the casket with a nod. Then JB stepped up. The cat on the closed casket lifted his huge head and made a sound low in his throat. JB pet him on his way to the open casket, and the cat quieted. But his stunning amber eyes remained fixed and guarded, almost as if he was trying to warn JB.

Nick and Toad helped JB climb into the casket. When he was on his back with his head resting on the pillow (which didn't feel nearly as fluffy and comfortable as it looked), Toad closed the lower half of the lid. Nick looked down at JB with a pleasant smile, and JB closed his eyes, as if he were merely going to take a brief nap.

Nick chuckled at the bravado and said, "Good-night, sweet prince." Then he brought the lid down.

The sound of the latch clicking into place seemed magnified in the tight dark space, and immediately JB began to silently count off the seconds. He couldn't hear anything outside the casket, not over the sound of the blood crashing at his temples. The seconds didn't pass like minutes or anything like that, but the longer he lay there, the more he began to believe that it was anything but a temporary situation. When I felt him clenching, I whispered gently, *Easy, easy does it, we're almost there*, and this seemed to relax him a little.

It was when we were approaching the one minute mark

that the first real pangs of panic began to rise like a vengeful spirit . . . and when we actually *passed* the one minute mark that he began to sweat. I kept telling him, *Don't open your eyes—whatever you do, don't open them*. But the more I tried to stop him from opening his eyes, the harder it became for him to resist the temptation. I tried to tell him that he'd counted too quickly, that it hadn't yet been a full minute, but he wouldn't listen. All he could hear was the sound of laughter drifting at him from someplace close by. Muffled and indistinct, but clearly laughter.

Then suddenly a voice was shouting, "That's enough. It's been over a minute. Open it!"

And another voice, much closer, saying, "I'm not so sure a minute will do. We might have to extend this little experiment . . . just to make sure we get the correct results."

This was followed by the sound of a scuffle, and then that voice again, so very close to the casket now, saying, "What do you say, Jake? Sixty seconds seems so trivial. How 'bout we go for sixty *minutes* instead? You think you can hold it together for that long?" Then the voice turned away, but it was still clear. "What do you guys think? Longer? We could take this thing down to the mausoleum and stick it in one of the slots and let him simmer there for a while, where no one can hear him scream."

"Hell, yeah!" another voice called out (I'm fairly certain it was Toad). "We can put his little buddy Jabona here in with him. They can keep each other company . . . screaming their heads off all night!"

Then the voice closest to the casket said, "You two get any bright ideas and you can join them."

JB guessed that this threat had been directed at Jonah's buddies from Planet Hollywood—Cory and Marc—neither of whom looked like much of a fighter.

Then the voice was close again. "Ready for your night-long rest in the mausoleum, Jake Swaggy?"

It was a bluff—I kept telling JB that, and for a moment it

seemed to calm him. But when he felt the casket being lifted and moved, he completely lost it. Suddenly he was slamming at the inside of the lid with his forearm, driving at it with all his might, kicking and screaming like a wild man, like a caged animal in full frenzy. It seemed to go on forever—clawing, kicking, punching at the inside of the lid, screaming every known obscenity (as well as a few made up right there on the spot). It just went on and on until I was certain our head would explode . . .

And then suddenly the lid popped open . . . and JB lay there looking pretty much the same as he had when he'd first climbed in and closed his eyes. His hair was sweaty and he looked both pale and flushed at the same time—but he hadn't moved an inch or made a sound the entire time he was in the casket.

All of the struggling and kicking and screaming had taken place *inside* his own mind. And it hadn't been just JB violently trying to break out—it had been *me*, as well. I had become just as terrified as he, if not more. And when Jonah finally broke free of Giancarlo and Toad and came to the casket, I could feel the rage surging throughout our body. Jonah helped JB climb out of the casket, and he kept saying, "I'm sorry, man. Are you all right? I'm so *so* sorry. Are you all right?"

JB left the basement without a word—both of us needed air.

Jonah caught up with him outside and said, "I swear to you I did not know *any* of this was going to happen. Dude, I am so *so* sorry." He put a hand on JB's shoulder and said, "Jesus, Jake, you're shaking all over. God, I am so sorry. Are you all right?"

JB nodded, but he couldn't stop shaking. He was trying to respond, to tell Jonah that he was all right and that he didn't blame him for anything, when Nick came out onto the porch with a fresh bottle of beer.

Nick opened the beer as he came down the steps, and with a grin of approval, he offered the bottle to JB. "You earned this one, kid. You lasted a whole three minutes without a peep. I really thought you'd crack and start screaming, but you're a straight-up badass. No hard feelings, okay?"

I'm pretty sure that JB would have accepted the beer and taken a swig to show that there were indeed no hard feelings. But that's not *my* way of handling things after some asshole locks me in a casket for three minutes and makes me believe that I'm going to spend the entire night tucked away in a mausoleum.

I took the bottle, but instead of taking a swig, I swung it at Nick's head. For a guy who'd been drinking and smoking out half the night, Nick had excellent reflexes and ducked just in time, so the only thing the bottle ended up connecting with was one of the porch's stone pillars. The trouble was that I'd swung the bottle with such force that when it hit the pillar, it shattered in a powerful explosion, sending shards of glass flying . . . one of which—a particularly long and thick shard— flew directly at Nick and lodged deep into his right shoulder, like one of those stars the ninjas throw in martial arts movies.

JB and Jonah were both staring at it in stunned fascination when Mason's voice came from the porch in a drunken slur. "Holy shit, dude . . . you're bleeding like a stuck pig."

Jonah snapped out of his stupor and reached for the shard of glass. Nick pulled back and shouted, "Don't!" Only it didn't come out exactly like a full-throated shout, but more like a half-choked cry.

"You can't just leave it in there, dude," Jonah said.

Nick winced with a sickly nod and said, "Yes. Yes, I can. If you pull it out, it'll really start bleeding." He winced again, afraid to even look, and said, "How bad is it?"

"Pretty bad," Jonah said, still gazing at Nick's shoulder in horrified fascination. "Your sleeve is like soaked. Can't you feel the blood on your arm?"

"Yes, I can feel the blood on my arm, you dumb-ass bitch!" Nick hissed through gritted teeth.

Mason said, "It's like all slick with blood, yo—it's like dripping down to your hand."

Nick's face looked ashen as he broke into a sudden sweat. "Okay," he said with effort, "don't say that word again."

Mason looked confused. "What? Blood?"

Nick let out a painful breath and whispered through clenched teeth, "I'm gonna kill him."

Jonah snapped, "Shut the hell up, Mace!"

Mason said, "What'd I do?"

By now the other guys had come up from the parlor and gathered on the porch, all of them looking stunned at the sight of Nick's bleeding arm, none of them willing or able to approach. JB was the first to snap out of his stupor. He called out to Cory and told him to get a towel or something. Mason mumbled something about not using one of his mom's towels. Nick said that somebody might have to take him to the emergency room, and this got all of the guys quiet really fast.

JB looked around. They were all pretty baked and none of them looked ready or willing to get behind the wheel. And Nick looked like he was about to pass out.

JB took the drawstring off his hoodie and looped it under Nick's armpit and over the shoulder. Then he pulled it tight and tied it off. He quickly folded his hoodie and used it to mop Nick's arm. Nick winced and let out a little moan as sweat dripped from his brow. JB told him to hold the hoodie under the wound, and then he helped Nick to the passenger door of the Jeep. He asked where the keys were, and Nick said they were in his hip pocket. JB fished them out and then helped Nick into the Jeep. He didn't stop to ask if any of the others were coming. He just went around to the driver's side, got in, and fired up the engine.

The last thing he saw as he backed out of the driveway was the almost comically surreal tableau of six baked guys staring back at him from the porch of the funeral home with stupefied expressions on their faces.

§

By the time we got to the emergency room, a little of the color had returned to Nick's face. JB was pretty sure the bleeding had stopped, or at least slowed considerably, but he stayed by Nick's side with an arm out to catch him just in case. Nick bypassed the desk and headed straight down this short hall to the left; when he stumbled, JB caught his good arm and draped it around his shoulder.

Nick mumbled, "I feel dizzy, dude."

JB told him that it was all good, that he was going to be all right, but when Nick looked up and saw a nurse approaching from the opposite end of the hall, he said, "Wanna bet?"

The nurse came to a sudden halt when she saw Nick and sighed, "Sweet Mary, mother of God, what now?"

It seemed like a strange thing for a nurse to say, and JB looked confused until Nick said in a strained voice, "Please, Mom, not now, it really hurts."

The nurse nodded as if she'd just heard the understatement of the year and said, "Yeah, I'll bet it does." And without turning her gaze from Nick's arm, she spoke to JB. "Take him into exam room D. I'll be there in a second."

JB took Nick into the exam room and helped him up onto the table, and the nurse—Nick's mom—returned before JB even had the chance to say something lame like, "Your mom works here?"

Her name tag said Lillian Rivera, RN, and JB was struck by two things at once: that Nick's mom wasn't black and that she looked more like a nurse on a TV show than a nurse in real life. He guessed she was in her early forties, but she was still very pretty, and even though she was dressed in loose-fitting maroon scrubs, he could tell that she had a nice body. She didn't have an accent except when she was muttering in Spanish, which she did a lot while removing the shard of glass from Nick's shoulder and cleaning the wound. By Nick's reaction to his mom's muttered curses, JB gathered that Nick understood at least enough Spanish to know that he was in deep trouble.

After she'd peeled back the blood-soaked hoodie and removed the shard of glass, Nick asked if it was going to need stitches (which seemed like a monumentally dumb question to me, but JB clenched his teeth to prevent me from making a smart-ass comment).

Nick's mom nodded and said, "Oh yeah. A lot."

Nick winced. "Tell me you're joking."

"I'm joking," she said. "It's going to take five or six stitches. You're just lucky it didn't sever any of the nerves in the brachial plexus."

"What would that do?" Nick asked, wincing again.

"Nothing good," his mom said as she finished cleaning the wound. "Now lie back."

"Mom, I'll pass out if I lay on my back."

"Good, it'll make it that much easier for me to do my job."

"Mom, I'm serious," Nick whined, "my head is spinning. I think I lost too much blood." His mom rolled her eyes. Nick moaned. "No, seriously, mom, shouldn't they give me like a transfusion or something?"

"Maybe a brain transfusion," she said absently as she filled a syringe.

"Can't you just do it while I'm—" Nick winced as she gave him the injection with what looked like an extremely long needle. "—sitting up, please, mom?"

"Oh, quit being a baby and lie down." She turned to JB. "Would you help him get his legs up there, honey?"

JB took hold of Nick's legs and hoisted them up onto the table, and even though he did this extra slowly and carefully, Nick let out an agonizing moan, and his mom rolled her eyes again. As he reclined on the exam table, Nick asked if there was any chance he might choke on his own vomit. His mom said not if he didn't vomit and told him to hold still.

JB was surprised when Nick reached up with his free hand and whispered the word "bro," but he took Nick's hand and held it tightly while Nick's mom stitched up the wound. While she worked, she asked Nick if he would care to tell her how he ended up with a shard of broken glass in his shoulder. For a second JB thought Nick might fold under the pressure and tell his mom the truth, but Nick kept it together and told her that he was messing around with the guys outside Mason's house and tripped and fell. He said he didn't even know the glass was there until he felt it stabbing into his shoulder. It was difficult to tell whether Nick's mom believed the story, but JB was impressed by Nick's delivery, especially with his head swimming and the pain and all.

After his shoulder was stitched and covered with a fresh square of gauze, Nick sat up and immediately swooned. His mom went to the nurses' fridge and got a can of Ensure. She shook it up, popped the tab, and told Nick to drink it slowly and stay put until he felt steady enough to stand. When she turned her gaze to JB, I receded to my corner of our collective consciousness (something in her eyes made me apprehensive), and Nick said, "This is Jake. He drove me here."

Nick's mom looked into JB's eyes, but it was impossible to tell whether or not she recognized him. All she said was, "It's nice to meet you, Jake. I appreciate your help. I take it you were the only one in any condition to drive?"

JB's cheeks flushed. He tried to look away but couldn't. Like Mali the casting agent, Nick's mom had a way of looking at you that compelled your attention. When he opened his mouth to speak, the sound caught in his throat.

"It's okay," Nick's mom said with an understanding smile. "I won't pressure you to rat out your friends. I already know what they're up to, even if they think they're pulling one over on me." Her smile vanished when she shifted her attention back to Nick. "But maybe *you* should consider your little brother, who looks up to you as an example."

Nick muttered, "He doesn't look up to me . . . and I'm not much of an example."

She sighed. "You're the only one he's got, honey. You just need to figure out what kind of example you want to set for him. He's eleven years old, and it won't be long before whatever he's absorbing sticks." She brushed her knuckles gently along Nick's cheek and said softly, "You don't have to be a superstar to make a difference in his life."

Nick made a soft sound somewhere between a sigh and a clipped laugh. Then he sat quietly, looking down at the empty can in his hands. JB remained quiet too, and for a while it felt as if time was standing still.

Finally, Nick's mom sighed and said, "Do you suppose you could go home and relieve the sitter?"

Nick nodded.

JB could see the guilt, mixed with a healthy dose of shame, in Nick's eyes, and in turn this made JB feel guilty because if he'd only been able to stop me from taking control and swinging that bottle at Nick's head, none of this would have happened.

Nick's mom looked at JB, and for a second it felt like she could read his thoughts. But she didn't come at him with accusations and fiery threats. She just looked tired, like she didn't have any fight left in her. She said, "It's pretty late. You should call your mom and let her know that you're all right. I'm sure she's worried about you."

Then she gave Nick a hug and kiss, and as he leaned into her embrace, he suddenly looked much younger than eighteen. When she told him that she loved him, he nodded and said softly that he loved her too.

JB was pleasantly surprised when Nick's mom gave him a hug too. But when she brushed his hair out of his eyes and thanked him again for helping out her son, JB felt even guiltier than before. Then Nick's mom was gone, and it was just JB and Nick alone in the brightly lit exam room, neither of them knowing what to say.

§

JB drove Nick home in the Jeep. Nick wanted to drive him back to the strip, but before we'd left the hospital, JB promised Nick's mom that he would make sure Nick got home safely. JB called for a cab when we reached Nick's place and then sat on the porch steps next to Nick while he waited for the cab.

For a while it was just like it had been back at the hospital, with the two of them sitting in complete silence, and JB figured that maybe it was a good thing. Then Nick spoke. His voice was soft and his eyes were focused on the street, but it was clear that he was speaking directly to JB.

"I used to want to be a pop star," he said. "When I was a kid, I used to think that I was gonna be the next Usher. I had a decent voice and I could dance, and I thought, 'That's gonna be me one day. *I'm* gonna be Usher.'" He let out a short laugh and stared off into the night for a long moment; then he said, "Braden—that's my kid brother—he was like seven at the time. He'd sit there and watch me practice my moves, and even when I'd screw the whole thing up, he'd look at me like I was a star. It didn't matter to him. He thought I was as cool as it gets. I kept at it for a couple of years, and I was getting better, but I still wasn't Usher. It didn't matter to Braden, but it did to me—I mean, if you can't be the best at something, why bother, right?"

He looked into JB's eyes pointedly before turning his gaze back to the street. JB remained silent, sensing there was more. After a moment, Nick continued.

"But I still kept going at it. I kept working at it every day. Every chance I got. And I was getting better, but still not good enough—not for me, at least." He paused, briefly. "And then one day something happened that changed everything." He paused again. "You know what that was?"

JB waited, but Nick remained silent. He didn't look angry or tense or anything like that. Just silent.

JB shifted uncomfortably and said softly, "What was it? What happened?"

Nick turned his head and looked directly into JB's eyes again. "You did."

Again there was no malice in his tone, no accusation in his gaze. He just looked like a guy stating a simple fact—one that JB made no attempt to refute.

It was quiet for a moment. Then Nick smiled and said, "I'll never forget the day Braden came running up to me when I got home from school. He was all excited, and he pulls me into the living room to show me this video on TMZ. And there you were with Usher, and they had all these video clips of you singing in your living room. And there I was, knowing that it was over. Braden was excited because if it could happen for a kid like you out of nowhere, then it could happen for me. But I knew it was never going to be me standing next to Usher on TMZ. I knew I wasn't gonna be *that* kid. I knew that I couldn't *learn* what you had. You're either born with it, or you're not. And I wasn't born with it."

JB's expression was so gravely sincere that Nick laughed— not a sneering laugh, just the gentle chuckle of one who knows the situation isn't nearly as bleak as it seems.

"Dude, it's all good," Nick said. "It's not like you shattered my dream or anything like that. It's more like you opened my eyes to a truth I'd been ignoring for a long time."

Nick gave him a friendly punch on the arm, and JB pushed a small smile, but the guilt in his eyes lingered. Nick didn't see it, because he'd already turned his gaze back to the night. But I saw it, and it set me on edge because I knew from painful experience just how easily complex emotions like sympathy and guilt could build a wall inside the host that would be difficult—if not altogether impossible—to scale . . . even for the most cunning and agile of *ids*, like me. Nonetheless, I remained patient and vigilant.

Nick said, "And anyway, it all worked out for the best

because about a year after I'd dropped the whole thing, I come home one day to find Braden sitting on the couch with my guitar, and he's playing it." He laughed again, nostalgically this time. "He's a lefty, like you, and so he'd taken all the strings off the guitar and restrung them so he could play it left-handed. Can you believe that? The kid was like nine years old at the time, and he did this all by himself. And there he is, playing this old guitar, and the sound coming out of it is beautiful. And he's singing one of the songs from your first album, and he has no idea that I'm standing there watching him, and he . . . " Nick's eyes became suddenly misty, but he pushed back against the emotion and smiled (I tried to steel JB's nerves, but JB was clearly moved, which only made it worse). " . . . he sounds like an angel. Can you believe that, bro? All that time I'm trying and trying to do something that I have absolutely no talent for, and here my kid brother ends up being a natural."

Nick's eyes shined with pride, and JB smiled.

"And he's good—I mean *really* good. I've been saving up for this Larrivee that he wants—the SD60RWI, I have that memorized." He uttered a short laugh. "I told him if he got all A's, I'd get it for his birthday. I've almost got it covered— I've been working my ass off, putting in extra hours." His eyes suddenly looked tired, like those of a much older person. "His birthday is tomorrow—I tried to make it in time, but . . . " He shook his head. "I told him it was going to have to be a late present, and he was so cool about it. I know kids who would have had a fit over something like that. But not Braden. He's not like that. He's . . . he's a good kid." He gave another short laugh and shook his head again. "Our mom is gonna have a fit because she thinks I'm saving up for college, but I know how much he wants that guitar, and I'm not gonna let him down."

The look in Nick's eyes gave JB a sudden nostalgic chill because it was the same look he'd seen in his own eyes count-less times while gazing into the mirror after brushing his teeth just before bedtime—back when stardom was still a distant dream and the world before us was filled with hope and infinite possibilities. It was the look that said *Nothing is going to stand in my way.* But it hadn't been JB giving that look to the mirror—it had been *me* inside the mirror giving that look to him. JB would have been happy if all we ever had was the YouTube fans. The money and the prestige, and the power that came with success didn't matter to him at all. For JB, it was all about the fans. And for Nick, it was all about his kid brother Braden.

"He's not like me," Nick said. "He's more like you." He smiled and added, "He's a little white boy too . . . well, not as white as you, but his dad was white, and so he looks like a white boy with a tan." He laughed. "He looks up to you like an idol. He knows all of your routines, all of your songs, and, no offense, he can do them every bit as good as you. He writes his own songs too, and they're really good."

JB smiled, and Nick smiled too. But then Nick's expression turned a little dark.

"He takes a lot of shit at school. Kids pick on him and call him a fag for liking you. It got so bad last fall that I wanted to go to his school—just to throw a scare into them, y'know? But he begged me not to because it would only make it worse. He's not a fighter like me. He's never caused any trouble like I have. He just does his thing and gets good grades and doesn't mess with anybody, and I don't want that to change . . . I don't want him to be like me. He's better than that. He has a chance to be like you, and I'll do anything I have to do to make sure that he gets there. Anything."

Nick shook his head gently, but his eyes still looked dark. JB didn't know what to say. And for a while, it was quiet. JB wanted to offer to go inside and meet Nick's brother, but he wasn't sure if that would be a good thing. It wasn't about blowing his cover—Nick already knew who he was, and JB got the feeling that Nick's mom had known who he was too. The real reason he didn't offer to go inside and meet Nick's brother was because he didn't want to take any more from Nick than he already had. He supposed that the kid might always be a fan of his, but he knew that one day the kid would realize (if he hadn't already) that his true hero was his older brother. And JB didn't want to impede that realization by making a surprise "guest appearance" on this night.

The cab finally showed up at a little after 1:00 A.M., and as it pulled to a stop at the curb, JB stood and held a hand out to Nick. Nick accepted his hand with a sad smile. JB was at the cab's back door when Nick called out to him, "Hey, man . . . I'm sorry about the coffin thing. I shouldn't have done that. It was a dick move, and you didn't deserve it."

JB looked back at him. He wanted to say, *Yeah, I did deserve it . . . for more reasons than you know.* But instead he just said, "It's all good, bro. No worries."

But it wasn't all good, and there were worries—all sorts of them.

I could feel something stirring within on the ride back to the Strip, but JB held it together until we were up in our suite at the Aria. He stood at the window in silence, gazing out at the dark sky. I wanted to say something, but I knew better than to intrude on the moment. He was thinking about everything that had happened over the past few days, but at the center of his thoughts was what had happened over the last couple of hours—the party, where he'd sung the Iron & Wine song; the funeral home, where he'd been locked inside a casket; the hospital, where Nick's mom had stitched up the cut on her son's shoulder; the porch outside Nick's house, where beyond one of those darkened upstairs windows lay a little boy, asleep and dreaming dreams that JB himself had once dreamt . . . completely unaware that his idol was down on the front porch having a chat with his older brother. And as JB's thoughts homed in on that sleeping boy, he could hear Nick's voice . . .

Braden—that's my kid brother . . . he's not like me . . . he's a good

kid . . . a lefty like you . . . looks up to you like an idol . . . and he's
good—I mean really good . . . he takes a lot of shit at school . . . kids
pick on him . . . he's never caused any trouble . . . and call him a fag
for liking you . . . you, bro . . . singing one of the songs from your
first album . . . just like you . . . and he sounds like an angel . . . like
you . . . and I don't want him to change . . . I don't want him to be
like me . . . he's better than that . . . he has a chance . . . a chance to
be like you . . .

JB's stomach clenched at the sound of those words echoing through our mind, and I cursed myself for ever swinging that beer bottle at Nick. Had I just controlled my temper and let it go, we would have left the funeral home and never met Nick's mom at the hospital or heard Nick's story about him and his kid brother on the porch. And JB's mind wouldn't have been poisoned with all this emotional crap.

Now that may sound a little overly dramatic to you, but that's exactly what it was like: a poison, slowly working its way throughout those parts of JB's consciousness that I simply have no control over—and it really pissed me off. All of my work was about to come undone by a random act of uncontrollable violence.

Okay, it wasn't all that random—I *wanted* to crack Nick's skull with that bottle. And it wasn't completely out of my control—I could have taken a moment to stop and think before lashing out like a madman. But come on, the guy locked us in a *casket!*

Of course, for JB, none of what Nick had done to *precipitate* the incident with the bottle mattered. JB has never been very good at holding grudges—that's always been *my* burden; he's much more of a "turn the other cheek/forgive and forget" sort of guy. What can I say? He's a mixed-up Pisces—with all that watery emotion flooding his conscience, it's a wonder he hasn't drowned the both of us already.

He stood at the window like that for a half hour, and I couldn't get near him. I just had to sit back and hope against hope that the dam wouldn't break. I guess I don't have to tell you that the odds weren't exactly in my favor, and I guess what happened next was almost inevitable.

JB picked up his phone and dialed the last number I wanted him to dial. I tried to get his finger to slide down the list to that sweet little brunette's number—she might have cooled off by then, and a little night visit from her could have possibly shifted JB's thoughts away from all the melancholy bullshit brought on by Nick's sob story. But he scrolled right down to "S" and clicked on the number there before I could stop him.

It rang only twice before a familiar voice came through the speaker and entered JB's ear like an invading force. I'm pretty sure that JB would have just hung up if only that voice had said something like "Where the hell are you?" or "How could you put everyone through this?" or "You'd better have a good explanation." But there was no accusation in the voice. Only concern. And an unexpected wave of emotion came crashing through JB's resistance at the first words spoken by that calm voice: "Are you all right?"

JB's eyes filled with tears, and he had to fight them back before he could speak. "I'm okay," he whispered.

"Well, that's good to hear," Scooter said gently. "You had us a little worried for a while there, kid."

JB nodded, pushing back against the tears that continued to threaten, and said, "I'm sorry."

His voice sounded so fragile that I wanted to burst forward and take control, but his resolve was more powerful than you'd think. He was determined to say what he had to say, and I was powerless to stop it.

There was a long period of silence in which Scooter patiently waited and I held my breath. Then finally JB got himself under control enough to speak.

"Could I ask you something, bro?" he said.

"Of course you can," Scooter said with infuriating compassion.

"What would happen . . . " JB stopped and forced back the lump in his throat. "What would happen if I decided to give it all up? What would happen if I just decided to quit tomorrow and walk away from it all?" He paused again to push back against another wave of emotion, but his voice cracked when he said, "Would you be mad at me, bro?" A hot tear fell down his cheek, and I winced. "Because I don't think I could take that, you know? I don't think I could take . . . disappointing you like that after all you've done for me, you know?"

The line was silent for a long moment, and then Scooter said softly, "No. I wouldn't be mad at you."

Now more tears began to fall, and Scooter's voice came through the phone in a gentle tone that only made JB's raw emotions swell even higher.

"Justin, if you're not happy and you don't want to do this anymore, I'll be behind you one hundred percent. You tell me what you want and I'll make sure that nobody tries to push you in any direction you don't want to go." Scooter paused, then said, "You tell me where you are and I'll come get you myself right now. No security, no press. Just me." He paused again, briefly. "Your mom and everyone here just wants to know that you're safe. Your mom has been scared sick that something has happened to you . . . but if you don't want me to tell her that we talked, I won't. Just tell me where you are and I promise you I'll come get you myself, and nobody needs to know . . . we can talk, and nobody needs to know . . . I just want you to be safe . . . I promise you . . . "

JB swallowed back the tears and said, "Can you promise me that little Braden will be safe? Can you promise me that the other kids at school won't pick on him and call him a fag? Can you promise me that you can keep him safe from all the crazy shit out there? Can you promise me that?"

Scooter said, "I don't know who that is, Justin. Is he a friend of yours from school? If you want me to, I can get in contact with him for you . . . if you give me his information . . . "

A sudden surge came from somewhere within—someplace

that even I didn't know of—and JB snapped, "Don't *dick* with me, Scooter."

"I'm not dicking with you, Justin. If your friend is in trouble and you want me to help him, I will. I'll do whatever I can . . . "

JB's tone shifted and he said softly, "You can tell my mom that I'm all right . . . you can tell her that . . . and tell her . . . tell her that I love her . . . would you tell her that for me, please?"

"Of course I will—"

"I have to go," JB said abruptly. "You tell my mom that for me."

"I will."

"I need some time . . . I gotta figure something . . . I have to go."

"Justin, listen, I—"

JB hung up the phone and turned off the ringer. Then he looked back to the window. But he wasn't looking at the view of the Vegas skyline anymore.

He was looking at the ghostly figure of me staring back at him from the darkened pane of glass.

He was done crying, but his body was still trembling a little when he said, "You've got one more day."

I didn't bother with a response, and he didn't wait for one, either. He just turned away from the window and headed straight for the toilet.

He made it just in time, too—a few seconds later, and he would have thrown up right there in the middle of our lavish suite.

THE LAST DAY

I can still recall this one time when JB was seven years old. We were at the park he loved to visit when life was still fresh and every new encounter was fascinating. At the center of this park there was a huge pond, and it was JB's favorite place because of the long wooden docks that extended into the water. He loved to sit on the docks with his legs dangling over the side and his chin resting in one of the X-shaped frames of the guardrail. He would sit like that for hours, watching the older boys race their motorized model boats across the water. Sometimes he would focus on their hands moving gracefully over the remote controls and dream about the day his own hands would be skillful enough to do the same. But mostly he just liked to watch the boats slicing through the water. As the waves parted at their bows, he would imagine that the miniature vessels were full-sized ships, guided not by teenage boys with remote controls but by men hoisting billowing sails as they cut across some far-off sea. Of course, these were not just any ships—they were *pirate* ships, complete with skull and crossbones flags flapping in the wind. JB would imagine these ships exchanging cannon fire as they raced to the far side of the world in search of hidden treasure. And he would imagine that he himself was *on* one of these ships—the fastest in the whole armada because he wanted to be the first to touch shore and plant *his* ship's flag on the soil above the buried treasure. And after the older boys had all taken their boats out of the pond and left to do other things that older boys do—when JB had the docks all to himself—he would race up and down the wooden planks, invisible sword in hand, ready to do battle with the Pirate King of the opposing ship.

And, of course, that's where I would come in.

I would rise from the water, a perfect replication of JB—at least physically—but there was always something a little darker about me, edgier, craftier, more cunning (which I supposed made me a natural for the part of the dastardly Pirate King of the Black Ship). And there on those docks we would fight for the treasure, skillfully wielding our invisible weapons, dashing from spot to spot, thrusting and parrying, locked in a passionate "duel to the death" (trust me, it doesn't seem quite so silly when you're seven years old and have tons of energy to burn). It would always end the same, with me being felled by JB's sword and JB crying out that he'd finally avenged the death of his father, the honorable Lord Rauhl. And after, the two of us would sit on the dock and gaze out at the water with bright and hopeful eyes fixed firmly on a glorious future that we would one day share.

It was on this one particular occasion—a warm and sunny day, the sort they write about in poems and literature—that JB and I shared what you might call an epiphany. He was skipping stones across the still water while I stood on the surface watching. I had said something about getting our own boat—a *real* boat—and sailing the seas, just the two of us. He laughed and said he couldn't do something like that because he was too young to go sailing by himself. I smiled and said that many young people had struck off on their own, like Jim Hawkins in *Treasure Island* and David Balfour in *Kidnapped*. JB laughed and said that those were just stories. I nodded and said, "Yes, but all stories are based on *some* truth."

He thought about it, but I could tell that he was still no closer to believing that *he* could ever be like either Jim Hawkins or David Balfour—they were both very brave boys who weren't afraid of adventure. He shook his head and said, *"You* could be like them, not me."

"Why not you?" I gently coaxed (even back then I was quite adept at smooth-talking him).

"I'm not brave like you."

"Sure you are," I said, working the old charm. "You're the bravest kid I know. Look at how you held it together when that idiot cousin of yours locked us in the toy box."

"I was scared," he said.

"Yeah, but you were brave too. You made it through the whole thing without panicking." I smiled a small sly smile. "Okay, you panicked a *little,* but you didn't completely lose it. You're braver than you think."

JB looked dubious. "That was you. You kept me from losing it."

"That's right," I said with a genuine smile, "because we're a team, you and I. We can succeed at anything we do together. If I'm not afraid, then you don't need to be afraid . . . and *I'm* not afraid of anything."

"Yeah, but you're older than me."

I looked at him for a moment and then said softly, "I won't always be."

For a second, I felt something close to melancholy tug at the place where my heart would be if, in fact, I were a real boy like JB. It was a painfully empty sensation that reminded me in no uncertain terms that I was *not* a real boy and, further, that my existence was entirely dependent upon my ability to keep JB dependent upon *me.*

I suppose something in my eyes spooked him because he flinched—just a slight twitch. Normally, I would have enjoyed this—even back then I liked being perceived as a dangerous character who might do something unexpected; if people are worried that you might snap, it keeps them from messing with you. Of course, JB wasn't the type of kid to mess with anybody. He just wanted to make people happy, even at his own expense. But he wasn't a pussy. And he didn't fear me (at least not in the manner that any other kid his age would have feared me, and rightly so). Despite my enigmatic nature, he trusted me, and he always came right out and said what he was thinking.

"What do you mean, you won't always be older than me?" He was smiling this curious smile, but his eyes looked serious. "What're you like Peter Pan or something?"

Until that very moment, it had never occurred to me that JB didn't fully grasp that I was as much a part of him as his eyes or his hands or his lungs, through which we both drew breath. Back when he was five, he used to refer to me as his "twin," and when he got caught doing something he shouldn't be doing, he would say that it was his twin's idea (which was certainly true—JB was clearly the follower back then, and I the leader). Most adults found this particularly amusing and would smile and ask why they couldn't see his twin, to which JB would reply, "Because he lives inside of me and only likes to come out when we're alone." When one of the more wily adults would ask how his twin got inside him, JB would simply reply, "I swallowed him."

It was a clever answer that never failed to draw laughter from the grown-ups. And it was more accurate than five-year-old JB could have imagined. He'd swallowed me all right—but like most things you shouldn't swallow, I knew that eventually I'd be coming back up.

As I stood on the surface of the lake on that warm and sunny afternoon of our childhood, I pondered his comment about me being like "Peter Pan or something," and I smiled and nodded and said, "Yeah, like Peter Pan . . . or something."

JB smiled in return, but I detected a touch of confusion in his eyes. My gaze shifted to the dock, where JB's shadow had begun to stretch out in the slanting sun, and with a sly smile, I said, "Like Pan's Shadow . . . "

The image of that shadow growing longer on the dock was still in my thoughts when JB woke very late on the third day of our little adventure—the night before had been so long and exhausting, both physically and emotionally, that he'd broken the Vegas curse and slept straight through the morning and well into the afternoon.

When he rose and stretched, I caught a glimpse of his eyes from the ghostly reflection in the wide window opposite the bed. There was no sign that he had any knowledge of the dream I'd been having just before he woke (which wasn't surprising in the least—though we share the same brain, we often have separate dreams). As he headed for the toilet to relieve himself, I couldn't help smiling a secret smile and thinking: *Pan's shadow is still flying free . . . and my sweet, trusting "Peter" hasn't caught up with me yet.*

This was it. My one last day to take the wheel and right our little floundering ship before we came crashing into the rocky shore at low tide. I wasn't upset that JB had slept away most of the day he'd promised me—it wasn't the *quantity* of time that mattered but rather the *quality* of it. And anyway, *my* little corner of our brain functions much better in the evening hours . . . when it's far more difficult to spot a shadow in action.

JB was showered and dressed and out the door by 5:00 P.M. My plan was to catch a bite to eat and then head straight for the casinos. But it didn't go quite that way, because JB insisted on making a stop before we did anything . . . and as things turned out, it was a most fortuitous stop.

We took a cab to this shop called Guitar Center, where they have tons of guitars, every brand and style you can think of. JB didn't do any browsing like he normally would have, because he already knew what he wanted. When the clerk, this heavyset guy in his late twenties with longish frizzy hair and a fluffy orange beard, asked JB if he could help him,

JB said he was looking for a Larrivee SD60RWI. The clerk, whose name was Sandy, nodded with a smile of approval and brought out the guitar. JB spent a few minutes picking out a case—he settled on an SKB hardshell—and when Sandy asked if he wanted to purchase a protection plan that would cover the guitar for up to five years, JB nodded.

While Sandy was ringing up the order, he smiled and said, "Man, I'm sure you get this all the time, but I gotta ask, are you . . . you know?"

JB returned the smile and shook his head.

Sandy laughed. "I didn't think so. But man, do you *look* like him! It's spooky. I'll bet you get that all the time, huh?"

At the sound of Sandy's laugh, a deep jovial chuckle, it struck JB that Sandy looked a bit like the comic actor Seth Rogen. But he didn't mention this to Sandy. He just nodded with a shy smile and said, "Every once in a while."

Sandy laughed that good-natured Seth Rogen laugh of his again and said, "I'll bet."

JB paid for everything in cash—almost four grand total (if he'd done this anyplace else, it would have likely raised suspicion, but in Vegas, a large cash purchase doesn't even raise a casual brow). He asked if the store did deliveries and before Sandy could answer, he added that he needed the guitar to be delivered to a local address by 7:00 P.M. and that the cost of delivery was not an issue. He peeled two one hundred dollar bills from his roll and laid them on the counter. For a moment, he was almost certain that Sandy was going to shake his head sadly and say that he couldn't help him out. But then Sandy turned and called out to one of the other clerks, "Bobby, I'm going on break. I'll be back in thirty."

JB gave him the address, and as Sandy wrote it down, JB asked him to add this message: "To Braden. A promise kept. Happy Birthday. With love from your big brother Nick."

"That's some birthday gift," Sandy said as he finished writing the message on the back of a Guitar Center card. "He must be the greatest kid brother ever . . . or you're like the greatest big brother ever."

Sandy chuckled, and JB smiled, grateful that Sandy didn't ask why he didn't just deliver the guitar himself. Sandy seemed to sense that possibly Big Brother Nick wasn't welcome at home, and JB figured it was best to let him think that.

Before he left with the guitar, Sandy turned to JB and said, "Why don't you stick around and browse for a while. I'll be back in like twenty—I drive like a maniac—and I can let you know how the kid reacts to it."

JB's tentative expression only made him look more like the prodigal older brother, which only made Sandy feel sad for him.

Sandy said, "Just hang out. I'll be back in no time."

JB thought about taking off after Sandy was gone, and I nudged him to follow through on that thought—the last thing I needed at this point was for the jolly fat guy to return with that big warm smile of his and start telling JB how little Braden's eyes lit up when he got his birthday present. I was on a mission here, and I didn't want JB's bleeding heart to gum up the works. But no matter how hard I tried, JB kept resisting me (like I said, he can be quite stubborn when he puts his mind to something). I'd actually managed to maneuver him pretty close to the exit, and with a little more effort, I'm pretty sure I could have gotten him out the door and back into the cab. But in the end I didn't have to strain myself, because out of nowhere fate decided to send the perfect jackass to do the heavy lifting for me.

We were standing by this rack of sheet music when this guy with these cool hazel eyes and short dark hair swept forward into a duck's-ass swish came up with this smooth grin on his face and said, "Hey, man."

JB looked up at him, and immediately I shoved forward, giving the guy the hard edge of our gaze that I normally reserve for paparazzi (if you've ever seen that picture of JB and Selena in his car—the one where she's covering her face, and he's flipping the bird at the paparazzi through the wind-shield—then you know the look I'm talking about . . . and yeah, that was all me, front and center, shooting those sweet daggers at those camera clicking pricks straight through JB's eyes . . . there's really only so much of that crap I can take before I see red, you know?).

Anyway, so the second I hit this guy in the music shop with the old hairy eyeball, he throws up his hands and chuckles like him and JB are old buddies and says, "Take it easy, bro. I come in peace."

I suppose that was supposed to be funny or clever or some such shit, but it only made him seem like more of a douche. He was one of those generically good-looking guys that assume everyone will just drop to their knees and open wide at the sight of a smooth grin and dreamy eyes. JB would have prob-ably just given him a friendly nod, like "no harm, no foul," but I wasn't in the mood, and so I kept the old eyes nice and hard and chilly.

That didn't stop him, of course (with guys like him, it rarely ever does). He just kept smiling that monkey smile of his and said, "I'm Patrick."

He held out his hand, and to my chagrin, JB shook it. He said he couldn't help but notice JB from across the shop and that he actually did a double-take because he couldn't believe his own eyes. I wanted to puke, but JB just stood there looking at this Patrick guy and waiting for the rest, which came right on cue.

"Man, I still can't believe it," Patrick said, shaking his head with that phony smile. "My little sister is like your big-gest fan."

I tried to roll JB's eyes on that one, but he stopped me. He continued to listen as Patrick went on and on about his little sister and how she was gonna freak when he told her how he ran into JB in Vegas. It seemed to go on forever. The guy just wouldn't shut up. On and on he went about all the posters his little sister had on the walls of her bedroom and how she listened to JB's songs all the time and how she had like tons of magazines with JB on the cover and how much she *loved* his perfume—I'm not kidding, this guy was like a total maniac. He kept touching JB's arm and smiling and saying that he couldn't believe that he was standing right the eff there with *J effing B* (he said it just like that too, substituting the F word with "eff" and "effing"). And no matter how much JB tried to smile politely and explain that he wasn't the guy Patrick thought he was, Patrick wouldn't let up. He just kept grinning and going, "Come on, dude, I *know* it's you. You just laid out four grand in cash for a left-handed guitar—I mean, like, duh!"

It wasn't until Patrick put his hand on JB's shoulder and drew close that JB could smell the alcohol on his breath and see the blurry look in his eyes. And by this point the guy was squeezing JB's shoulder in a sort of massaging gesture and saying extra softly, "It's okay, dude, I'm not gonna tell anybody. I know how it is. Just do me a solid. Gimme an autograph for my kid sister. She *really* loves you, man. She's like your biggest fan. Just lemme take a picture with you—it'll make her day . . . it'll make her *year*. You gotta do that, bro. For a fan, you know? Right?"

JB tried again to explain that the guy was mistaken, and that's when Patrick put his other hand on JB's cheek and gave him a hard gaze. "Look, man, don't be such a little bitch. I'm asking you *nicely* here. You don't want to disappoint your biggest fan, right? So, take the stick out of your ass and do a bro a solid here, all right?"

As if that wasn't enough of an insult, Patrick made the added mistake of patting JB's cheek, like a grown-up would do to a little kid, only a little harder. It didn't sting or anything, but it triggered a response that JB could *not* prevent.

In a flash, I surged forth and shoved the guy backward.

It was so sudden and unexpected that he stumbled and almost fell over. I gave him the dark edge of JB's eyes and said, "You need to step off, bro. Seriously. Or there's gonna be consequences."

Patrick raised a hand and nodded while averting his gaze. "All right, I hear you, my bad. I shouldna done that. I'm really sorry, man. I just . . . I only wanted an autograph for my sister. I'm a little messed up here, and I shouldna done that. Boundaries, dude. I crossed the line, and I'm sorry." He looked up, and gone was all the swagger and bravado; he just looked like a guy who'd had a little too much to drink and was ready to chill. He nodded again and said, "I don't suppose you'd consider doing that autograph for my little sister—she really is your biggest fan."

I kept JB's eyes on him, hard and dark. He nodded and waved it off like maybe it wasn't such a great idea after all and walked away.

I held JB's gaze firm as Patrick went to the other end of the shop and disappeared behind a row of guitars. I was about to turn to the door and force JB to make a hasty exit when a familiar voice said, "Justin?"

I don't know why I did what I did next (maybe it wasn't even me who did it—maybe it was just an instinctive reaction by JB), but I turned, and there she was, the last person either of us expected to see—certainly not in the middle of a music shop in Vegas on a Thursday night. For a second, JB thought it was an illusion, a waking dream, and he blinked comically. But the vision didn't change. It was her. It was Miley (yes, *that* Miley, *the* Miley), and she was standing not ten feet away from us. I actually had the time to think *What are the odds?* before she started walking toward JB.

She had a big smile on her face, and she opened her arms for a hug as she said, "What in the world are *you* doing here . . . ?"

But she stopped short of the hug when she got close enough to see the look in JB's eyes. It was as if maybe she'd been confused—as if maybe JB wasn't who she'd first thought he was. This was likely due to the fact that I was still front and center, the razor-sharp edge of my gaze still burning through JB's eyes. For a moment, it was as if Miley was frozen with indecision. I didn't wait for her to recover. I just turned JB's body, and we walked out of the shop.

What happened next all came in a surreal blur, like shots from a movie, with several frames removed to make the action seem stilted and cool, but there was nothing cool about it.

JB stepped outside and took a deep breath of fresh air as he headed for the cab. Miley came from the shop and called out to him. He stopped just shy of the cab, but not because of Miley—he'd heard her calling his name, but it was the vision in front of him that had halted his steps. Standing on the sidewalk were the two girls we'd met at Blossom on our first night here in Vegas. Krystal, the redhead, and Diana, the brunette. And JB just stood there, staring at them, unable to move. Then, on his periphery, he saw someone come from the music shop and push past Miley, and he heard Miley shout, "Hey!"

But JB didn't turn in time, because his eyes were still locked on Diana's. Then suddenly Diana's eyes got huge, and in a split second, JB's head exploded with pain. He staggered to his knees, one hand on the pavement and the other holding the back of his head—and somewhere in the mix of all of that, he heard a voice say, *"Don't you ever dis me, you stuck-up little prick!"*

Then his head was spinning, and Miley was shouting, "Hey! Hey, stop that guy!"

But the guy was running down the block, and JB didn't have to look up to know that it was Patrick, the drunk guy who'd wanted an autograph for his kid sister.

JB's head was still throbbing (Patrick's fist had caught him just behind the right ear) when he heard a car squeal to a stop and then several voices all speaking at once.

"Jake, are you all right?" That was Diana, and she was crouched down by him with one hand on his shoulder.

"Justin, look at me. Can you hear me?" That was Miley. She was crouched down too and had a hand on his other shoulder.

"Holy shit, Nick! What the hell happened?" That was Sandy, the store clerk who'd just screeched to a halt and bolted from his car—he was pretty fast for a heavyset guy.

Then they were all helping him up and asking him if he was okay and stuff like how many fingers could he see them holding up, and one of them said something about taking him to a hospital, but JB shook his head and said no. Then there was something going on between the girls—something about his name—Miley was asking the redhead why she was calling JB "Jake," and the redhead was looking at Miley like she was nuts, and Diana was just staring at JB in stunned disbelief.

Then Sandy was asking JB if he was all right, and when he referred to JB as "Nick," all of the girls looked confused. But JB didn't seem to notice. He asked Sandy if he'd delivered the guitar, and Sandy said he did. He said that the kid was ecstatic, that he'd never seen a kid that happy before. He said he took a picture of the kid with the guitar, and he fished his phone out of his pocket to show JB. The misty look in JB's eyes must have looked to Sandy like that of a proud older brother, but in fact, this was the first time JB had ever laid eyes on Nick's kid brother Braden. He was as Nick described him: a white boy with a good tan, but even so, JB could see the resemblance the kid bore to his real older brother, Nick. And looking at that face, filled with such joy over the gift his big brother had promised to get him, JB felt a powerful wave of emotion swell from within.

Sandy put a hand on JB's shoulder and said, "He told your mom he couldn't wait for you to get home from work so he could thank you, dude." He paused and then said confidentially, "I really think you should go see him. Your mom didn't look mad at all. She looked like she was really proud of you. I know it's not my place, but you should go see your brother on his birthday. That kid really loves you, man."

Sandy squeezed JB's shoulder gently and asked again if he was okay, and JB nodded. But he wasn't okay, and after Sandy headed back into the store, JB put a hand to the back of his head where Patrick had sucker-punched him. It still hurt but nowhere near as bad as the pain in his heart. He felt as if he could just sit on the curb, put his head in his hands, and let it all out. But if he did that, he knew the girls would just come to his side to coddle him and soothe it all away, and that's not what he wanted. He didn't want to be babied and told that everything would be all right. He didn't want their sympathy—he'd had enough of that to last a lifetime.

He wanted something else. He wanted to lash out and strike hard, the same way Patrick had. Only he wouldn't run afterward like a chickenshit little drunk. And he wouldn't strike from behind either with a cheap shot sucker punch. He would face his opponent with a clear eye and head-on. He was ready and willing to meet his destiny. But there was only one path that could take him there . . . and that path was only accessible through me.

He headed for the cab, and Miley followed, calling out his name, but he didn't turn back. Just before he closed the door on Miley, he could hear Krystal, the redhead, saying, "Who does that little skank think she's fooling with that phony accent? Like anyone would actually believe that she's Miley Cyrus. Riiiight."

Through the back window of the cab JB could see Diana standing on the sidewalk. She was still staring at him, and he could see in her eyes that she did not agree with her friend's sarcastic assessment at all. He could see that Diana's eyes were finally open to the truth. He could see now, when it was far too late, that Diana *believed*.

As the cab pulled away, JB spoke to me in the privacy of our mind, and there was no mistaking the gravity of his tone.

Your call, bro. Whatever you want, count me in.

§

The casino's lights blazed like flaming embers against the dark sky as the cab pulled up to the entrance, but JB didn't seem to notice anything out of the ordinary. He just got out of the cab and headed straight for the entrance, where this tall guy dressed in evening attire held the door open with a welcoming smile and said, "Good evening, sir. Please let the *maître d'* know if there is anything you require."

JB nodded in response, ignoring the distant signal from the rational center of his brain that something was out of place. Inside, the air was cool and refreshing, and we were immediately swept into the belly of the casino, which was pulsating with action. Every table was loaded with players, all of them beautiful and young and happy. The surrounding energy was electrifying. Invigorating. *Alive.* The hypnotic music of slot machines, spinning wheels, shuffling cards, and riffling chips invaded JB's senses like an intoxicating elixir and drew him deeper into the casino, where he sat down at our first table of the night. The dealer didn't ask to see his ID. When JB took out his roll to lay some cash on the table, the dealer blushed and with a polite smile said, "No need for that, sir. Your credit is good here."

JB looked slightly wary as he put his money back in his pocket, but he accepted the tall stack of chips the dealer pushed across the felt. He was still eying the dealer curiously when a cocktail waitress appeared and offered him a drink, which she referred to as an *"apéritif."* As he accepted the drink, JB was struck by the waitress's beauty. She was a lovely girl with dazzling eyes and sensuous lips, and he could scarcely take his eyes off her. She smiled a beautiful smile that set JB's heart to racing and wished him luck before she moved on with her tray of drinks. Then the dealer started firing cards from the shoe with lightning-fast precision . . . and the winning commenced.

By the time we'd left the first table, JB's stack of chips had grown so tall that the pit boss had to tally the amount and draw up a receipt for JB to give to the cashier. But he didn't go to the cashier. He simply moved on to another table, where another cocktail waitress appeared, even more lovely than the first. She offered JB an *apéritif*, and he drank it down in a single swallow, which drew cheers from the other players at the table. JB smiled shyly at the unexpected approbation of these strangers, but secretly he enjoyed it. He enjoyed being part of this happy crowd of players with their smiling faces and sparkling eyes. He enjoyed being in a place where there was no pressure, no expectations, no worries. Just good times all around, and when he accepted another drink from the waitress, he raised his glass to the approval of the crowd. And as the cards began to flow and the chips began to mount, JB felt better than he had in a very long time.

It went on like this at every table we joined—roulette, craps, blackjack, pai gow, let it ride, no-bust 21, baccarat—all winners, happy faces, lovely cocktail waitresses, smiling dealers. And with each triumph, JB became more and more confident, trading his shy smile for some genuine swagger as he dominated each game and led the charge. And the other players all followed him into victorious battle. All winners, no one left behind, because Swaggy had the sweet swagalicious moves, and Swaggy always takes care of his crew.

He had played nearly every table game (and even hit the jackpot on this one slot machine—with a single pull of the lever, no less) when something caught his eye at the far end of the casino. An area that had seemed just out of his reach all night, for every time he'd so much as glanced in that particular direction, a waitress or a floor manager or another player immediately appeared and guided him to another table, where the allure of all those flowing cards and rolling dice and spinning wheels and mounting chips proved an insurmountable distraction. And this time was no exception.

The moment his gaze was drawn to that area at the far end of the casino, a girl appeared at his side and tugged at his arm, telling him that he simply *had* to come with her to the roulette table, where Red 23 had hit sixty-six times in a row, and she was absolutely *positive* that it was going to go for six hundred more! The girl was standing close to JB, her breasts brushing against his arm, her lips close to his ear, one soft and delicate—*facile*—hand stroking his hair.

But this time JB's gaze could not be averted. Because this time something was *different* about that area at the far end of the casino. As before, he could see the single table down there, positioned beneath an ambient light. Only, now the table wasn't empty. It was occupied by a young woman who looked vaguely familiar to JB. A young woman who was more beautiful than any of the stunning-looking waitresses who'd been bringing him drinks all night. And she was sitting at that lone table at the far end of the casino as if patiently waiting for someone to take the seat opposite her.

The girl at his side was still trying to coax JB into joining her at the roulette table when a young floor manager in a tuxedo shirt and vest appeared. He was tall and handsome, with a hard jawline and piercing blue eyes that seemed incongruous with his pleasant smile. His formal attire did nothing to conceal his broad shoulders and prominent chest; he looked like a high school jock at the prom—that smug sort of prick who had no compunction about stepping on the weaker kids. He eyed JB and said politely, "Perhaps you would care to join this young lady at the roulette table, sir."

I regretted putting those words into the floor manager's mouth almost instantly—even the most clever and gifted of *ids*, such as myself, can overplay a hand every now and then. In retrospect, I should have never brought the jock-like floor manager into it in the first place. I probably should have just projected the image of another girl—*ten* other girls, if necessary—to help lure JB away from that table at the far end of the casino. Though, I'm fairly certain nothing would have worked—the allure of the lovely young woman waiting for someone to join her at the lone table was just too powerful for

JB to resist. For a moment, I considered the idea of making the jock floor manager morph into a friendlier form (when you're operating on the inside of someone's consciousness, there's no limit to the tricks you can play on their eyes). But in the end, I let it go (I am, after all, a highly adaptable entity and know how to pick my battles). So the floor manager and the girl simply watched with cool gazes as JB walked away from them and headed for the one table in the casino that I'd been work-ing extra hard to keep him away from all night . . . because, like any competent *id*, I know there are certain areas of the psyche that are best left unexplored.

JB sat at the little heads-up poker table and nodded to the young woman sitting opposite him. She had blonde hair and lovely blue-grey eyes, the sort that look right into you with unflinching sincerity, like the eyes of a trusted older sister. As JB met her gaze head-on, he felt a little shiver. But not a bad one. It was the sort of shiver you get when you feel the onset of *déjà vu*. A good shiver, one that tells you it's okay to let your guard down, that everything will be all right if you trust your instincts and go with the moment. But familiar as she seemed, JB still couldn't place her face—hard as he tried, he couldn't remember where he *knew* her from. Even when she offered her name, which was Marilyn, some door in his memory refused to open. It wasn't like it was jammed or locked (like the time JB and I locked that producer in a closet on the set of *CSI* ;-), but more like the knob was being held in a vice grip from the other side . . . you know, like when your older brother has you trapped in a dark room, and no matter how hard you try to turn the knob, it won't budge, because his grip is way stronger than yours. I know that *sounds* like torture, but believe me, sometimes older brothers have good reasons for locking their younger brothers in dark rooms. Sometimes they have *very* good reasons, if you catch my drift.

When Marilyn introduced herself, she gave him her real name (I tried to cut her off, but I couldn't get my hand on that doorknob before she'd spilled it), and JB returned the gesture, offering *his* real name. It was sort of a no-brainer, considering that both Marilyn and the dealer already knew who JB was anyway. Marilyn knew him for reasons that were still hidden behind that closed door in his memory, and the dealer knew him because the dealer happened to be the guy who almost signed JB before Usher swooped in with the more enticing offer. The dealer's nameplate read: JT, and his normally curly blond mop was shaved on the sides and swept back straight.

A cart loaded with racks of chips arrived while JT was shuffling the cards, and the attendant who'd brought the chips said, "Your winnings, Mr. Swaggy."

JT the dealer smiled as he continued to shuffle the cards, and JB blushed. Being called "Mr. Swaggy" in front of *anyone* who knew his true identity would have been embarrassing enough, but it was only made worse with JT sitting right there, smiling that insufferably sly smile of his. JB's embarrassment was compounded by the fact that Marilyn had but a modest stack on the table while he was practically swimming in chips. He needn't have worried, though. His luck was about to take a sharp turn.

JT dealt the cards and spread each flop with cool precision and a neutral expression, just like one of those professional dealers you see on *Poker After Dark*—the guy is one suave bastard, as smooth as they come (to be perfectly honest, I wouldn't have minded being *his id* one bit . . . and *had* I been, I'd have let those Hollywood phonies have it with both barrels for not giving him the Oscar for *The Social Network*—the stingy posers could have at least thrown him a *nomination*—what a joke!).

JB played well—surprisingly well, in fact. He folded crap, raised appropriately on solid hands, and read the community cards on the board with amazing accuracy. The trouble was this: no matter the strength of his hand or how well he played it, Marilyn kept beating him with these unbelievable lucky flops and repeated miracle river cards. JB would go in strong with pocket Aces or Kings, and Marilyn would call with crap like Nine-Deuce off . . . and then hit trip Nines or Deuces on the board to give her quads. JB would hit an Ace-high flush only to see Marilyn pull a low-end *straight* flush with runners on the turn and river.

And on and on it went, just like that, hand after hand, until eventually, they had to bring in another cart just to stack all the chips Marilyn had taken from JB. And as he went deeper and deeper into the hole, JB began to feel this nervous energy coursing throughout his body. The sensation was so strong and rapid that I could actually *feel* him trembling. At first, I thought it was me causing this internal agitation—my anger can be incredibly fierce at times. But there was something *different* about it. It felt somehow contained. *Controlled.* It was as if JB was having some sort of cathartic internal explosion, and to be perfectly honest, it actually had me a little nervous.

And the magical hands just kept coming. If JB hit two pair, Marilyn hit a set; if he hit a set, she hit the straight; if he had the straight, she had the flush; if he caught the flush, she crushed him with the full boat; if he had the boat, she sank it with quads. What made it even worse was that a crowd had gathered—practically everybody in the casino—to witness JB's downfall. And worse still was that the surrounding speakers were cranked up and spilling out Lady Gaga's infamous "poker" anthem . . . which perfectly underscored Marilyn's complete domination of JB because, for all his effort, he could not read her poker face.

And the hits just kept on coming, over and over, but no matter how bad his defeat, JB held his tongue and kept on playing, hand after hand after hand of bad beats and outrageous losses . . . right up until this one hand where he hit quads on the flop with his pocket Aces.

For a moment, everything froze, and time seemed to stand still. Then JB looked up from his cards and gazed directly into Marilyn's eyes. As before, she looked beautiful and composed . . . but there was something in her eyes, something very deep, almost hidden . . . a quality of sadness that tugged at his heart . . . and just for a second, JB almost thought he had it—that elusive memory he'd been reaching for when he'd first laid eyes on her sitting alone at this table. But then it was gone, and his thoughts were back on the incredible hand he was holding: the Ace of Diamonds and the Ace of Spades, while out on the board in the three-card flop was the Ace of Clubs and the Ace of Hearts, along with an innocuous Deuce of Spades.

He thought about it for a moment longer.

There were only two possible hands that could beat him: a straight flush (in this particular case, Ace to Five or Deuce to Six, suited) and the mother of all hands, the unbeatable royal flush (Ace to Ten, suited). For Marilyn to take him with either, she would not only have to be holding suited miracle cards in her hand; she would also need to hit running miracles on both the turn and the river—and even with her incredible run of luck, *that* was highly unlikely. The odds were completely against her. Outside of the biggest bullshit miracle ever pulled off in a single hand of poker, there was simply no way that she could possibly beat quad Aces.

And still JB hesitated.

Seconds spilled into minutes. The crowd was deathly silent. The music had stopped.

Then JB said, "I'm all in."

And without hesitation, Marilyn said, "I call."

JB turned over his cards. A rolling murmur of awe spread through the crowd of spectators—even JT the dealer looked impressed. Marilyn's expression remained neutral, as if JB had turned over nothing more than a mere pair of Deuces instead of a soul-crushing pair of Aces. When she turned over *her* cards, JB's heart began to thunder so loud that he was certain the surrounding crowd could hear it.

Marilyn's cards were the King and Queen of Hearts, which put her two miracle cards away from the royal flush.

A powerful wave of blood was crashing at JB's temples like a tidal wave. At the same time Marilyn's expression remained perfectly composed, as if *she* were the one who had *him* dominated instead of the other way around (of course, with her amazing run of luck, you could hardly blame her). The crowd waited with eager—almost hungry—eyes, like a pack of wolves ready to pounce.

JT the dealer thumped the table, peeled a burn card off the top of the deck, and then took the next card and laid it on the table beside the flop in the turn position. And the crowd reacted with stunned gasps and nervous chuckles of disbelief.

It was the Jack of Hearts.

Now Marilyn was only *one* card away from the royal flush.

JB shook his head in disbelief at the suddenly very real possibility that his quad Aces could be taken down by a miracle royal flush, and he turned to JT the dealer and said, "Seriously, bro? You're gonna do me like that?"

JT's poker face remained as solid as Marilyn's.

JB said, "Is it because I went with Usher instead of you? Are you still pissed about that?"

JT allowed a slight shrug, with just the hint of a sly smile, but he remained silent.

JB sighed and shook his head again like he couldn't believe any of this was actually happening. I held my breath as that thought passed through his corner of our mind—but then something clicked. A scarcely audible sound, echoing from someplace deep inside our consciousness, but distinct. Like a key turning in a lock . . . and I could feel that doorknob start to slip in my grasp.

The knob made a complete turn, and the door fell open— just a crack—the moment JT the dealer laid the river card on the table.

It was the Ten of Diamonds, which gave Marilyn a straight, but *not* the royal flush. JB's quads had won the all-in pot.

The crowd was overjoyed (and visibly relieved) at the result. But JB was scarcely concerned because at the very same moment the last card hit the felt, something fell from the dark space high above and landed on the center of the table. At first

JB thought it was a feather, but when he looked closer, he saw what it really was: a damp lock of hair, freshly cut, just like you'd see on the floor of a salon . . . or a bathroom if you were getting a home haircut.

His eyes narrowed sharply, and suddenly he was pulling on that door in our mind, pulling with all his might to get at the memory locked inside that dark and secret room I'd been working to keep him out of all night.

As the door creaked open on its rusty hinges, the sound of scissors, clipping blithely away, flooded our collective consciousness. Images followed fast: damp locks of hair whispering softly along the sleek black beautician's cape and falling to the floor.

Then, in a series of rapid flashes, JB could see himself as a boy, perhaps nine or ten years old, looking at his new haircut in the mirror. He was smiling at the way it swept across his forehead, but still he was unsure. Then the beautiful girl who'd just given him the haircut was standing behind him, with her hands on his shoulders and her cheek against his, and she was smiling and telling him that the new haircut was his "trademark" and that one day people would recognize him by it. The girl was ten years older than him, and secretly he had a crush on her, which is why he'd agreed to let her cut his hair, even though she hadn't yet graduated from beauty school.

She had been his favorite babysitter; he remembered that now. She had been really sweet and never tried to sneak boyfriends over. She had always given him her full attention and played games with him, like Monopoly and Clue and Uno. But his favorite had been Idiot Poker, where you placed one of your own cards on your forehead for your opponent to see. He remembered that she would always let him win, no matter how good her hand. He remembered that she often dyed her hair different colors and how it made her look like a different person each time. He remembered thinking about her as he lay awake in his bed at night. And when he finally drifted off to sleep, he would dream of the day that he would be old enough to marry her because she was the prettiest, sweetest, most sincere girl in the whole world. He had been absolutely certain that when he grew up, she would fall as deeply in love with him as he already had with her. He would take care of her and protect her just the same as she had done for him. And he would always let her win at Idiot Poker. Even if he had the better hand, he would let her win.

JB looked across the poker table at Marilyn, and he could see her now for the first time. Really see her. And she was just as lovely as he remembered. Her eyes were misted with tears, and she was smiling because she knew that he recognized her now. And her smile broke his heart because he realized she hadn't come here to beat him and take all his winnings. He realized that she had come from the far reaches of his memory to *protect* him, just as she always had when he was a little boy.

With a sudden surge of strength, JB turned to the dealer and said, "Run it again."

All of the chatter and celebration at his recent victory stopped at once, and all eyes were suddenly on JB, frozen in expressions ranging from disbelief to outright disdain.

JT said, "Are you sure you want to do that, sir?"

JB said flatly, "Run it again."

JT moved the turn and river cards up on the felt and drew two new cards. The first was the Five of Clubs, which changed nothing. But the second was the magic card JB was looking for: the Ten of Hearts, which gave Marilyn her royal flush, which, along with JB's win on the first run, split the pot between them, so there was no winner and no loser.

As a collective groan rippled through the astonished crowd, the *maître d'* appeared, along with the young jock-like floor manager, who looked like he was prepared to get physical if necessary. When the *maître d'* asked if there was a problem, JT the dealer explained what had happened. The *maître d'* smiled politely and told JB that the house rules did not allow second runs. JB was about to debate the issue but suddenly shifted gears and asked a question the *maître d'* was not expecting.

"What is this place?" he said.

The *maître d'* bristled but recovered quickly and said with an air of pride, "This is The Shangri-La, sir."

JB said, "I've never heard of it. It's not on any of the maps. How long has it been here?"

The *maître d'* chuckled softly; the crowd joined him. The jock floor manager gave a smug smile that bordered on a snarl.

The *maître d'* said, "Oh, the Shangri-La has *always* been here . . . just as *you* have always been here, JB." He smiled politely and added, "Perhaps you would care for another *apéritif?*" He snapped his fingers, and at once several cocktail waitresses appeared, each with a tray of drinks.

JB stood. The jock floor manager's jaw tensed. The *maître d'* suggested that everyone remain calm.

JB shook his head and said, "This isn't real. None of you are real."

The *maître d's* features shifted, and his eyes looked suddenly dark and tense. The jock floor manager's nostrils flared. The expressions on the faces of the surrounding crowd no longer looked so warm and friendly.

The *maître d'* spoke purposefully. "We are very much real, Mr. Swaggy. And we serve solely at your everlasting pleasure, sir. The Shangri-La is your *home,* and we shall go to any lengths to make certain that you always feel welcome . . . so that you may never wish to leave."

JB shook his head again. "I wish to leave right now," he said, working hard to mask the tremor in his voice.

"I'm afraid," said the *maître d'* in a careful tone, "that we cannot allow that, sir."

"I want to leave right now," JB said flatly.

"You're overwrought, sir." The *maître d's* eyes grew darker still. "You should really have another *apéritif* and relax. There are so many more games for you to play, more winnings to be had—remember how you loved it so? The thrill of the blood racing through your veins . . . the triumph of your victory . . . the cheering of the crowd, your adoring fans . . . so many pleasures we can afford you, sir, if you will only allow us . . . "

JB looked at the jock floor manager, who seemed to morph before his eyes, and suddenly it was no longer the jock floor manager he saw. It was the wax statue he'd seen the day before at Madame Tussauds—not the Sid Vicious sculpture, but the one he'd *imagined* while gazing at the Sid Vicious sculpture. The one that looked just like him with the new haircut and all the tattoos. And suddenly this sculpture came to life, and it was surrounded by girls, groping at its half-naked body— but this vision only made JB's stomach turn because as the girls continued to grope the living sculpture, it began to melt, transforming it into a hideous creature, like something out of an old horror film, or a nightmare.

JB blinked, and the sculpture was gone. In its place was the jock floor manager, who made a fist with one hand and cupped it with the other while giving JB the dark edge of his purposeful gaze, as if to say: *You want out of here, kid—you're gonna have to go through me.*

JB shot a glance at JT the dealer, who gave him a scarcely perceptible nod—and in that brief moment JB felt really bad about turning down JT's offer and going with Usher; he knew that it was just business and that there were no hard feelings, but it made him feel really bad just the same.

What happened next took even *me* by surprise because JB just isn't a physically aggressive guy—at least not without some prodding from me (but like I told you, even the most wily and perceptive of *ids* can be caught off guard by a willful and motivated host, especially when said host kicks into survival mode). It may have started with that surreptitious nod from JT (helpful little dealer that *he* turned out to be), but what really gave JB the courage to act was the look he got from Marilyn, his former babysitter and creator of his "signature hairstyle." Once she gave him that look—the look that said "go for it"—JB was ready to do battle, and damn the consequences.

That's when all hell broke loose at the imaginary casino I'd spent days constructing inside JB's subconscious. All of my hard work gone to shit. And all due to a cheap memory of good times with a girl he should have long since forgotten (don't get me wrong here—she was a hot babe and well worth remembering, but she was also a meddlesome bitch who cost me an early victory lap at the old Shangri-La, so forgive me for not getting all weepy-eyed with emotion over those sweet memories of her from the good old days of popcorn and board games).

It went down in a flash. JB reached into the circle of trays the waitresses held out to him, but instead of taking one of the many glasses filled with the intoxicating elixir, he slipped his hand underneath the trays and brought it up hard, sending the drinks flying—straight into the face of the jock floor manager. Then immediately, he turned and broke through the stunned crowd.

The floor manager recovered quickly and reached with a long arm to grab JB by the back of his jacket—he almost caught him too, but just as he was turning to make his move, JT the dealer stuck out his leg, and the floor manager tripped and went crashing to the floor. His face came up bloody, but his eyes were on fire as he pointed at JB and uttered an ear-splitting shriek that sounded like the cry of a banshee or some other fabled creature of the night. Instantly, the surrounding crowd was whipped into a frenzy. With their faces no longer human, their eyes like shining gems, their mouths stretched wide, emitting that same ear-splitting shriek of the floor manager, they raced after JB, some of them on all fours, like a pack of wild animals, hell-bent and hungry.

JB ran through the casino, desperately searching for the exit as the tables behind him exploded, sending chips and cards flying everywhere. He didn't need to look over his shoulder to see the cause of these explosions—the bone-crushing blows of his pursuer's bodies colliding with the tables in their path rang as clearly in his ears as the accompanying shrieks. He had no desire to see the horrifying creatures that could collide with solid wood tables like that and keep going. So he just kept going too. As fast as his legs could carry him. But the casino just seemed to go on and on forever. Endless rows of tables—and slot machines whose fronts were all lit up with jackpots while their metal maws spilled tons of coins across his path, making his escape route more treacherous.

JB skidded across a shiny river of coins as he rounded one corner. His eyes lit up with hope when he saw the huge double doors at the far end of the towering row of slot machines. As he raced for the exit, the shrieking became louder and closer, and the sound of exploding slot machines and raining coins followed. A cold sweat broke over his body when he realized the creatures had shifted course and were now using their bodies to break through the barrier of slot machines on either side of his path to prevent him from reaching the exit. He didn't know if he could make it. He was out of breath, and his trembling legs were on the verge of giving out, so at the last moment, he tilted back and slid across the surface of the coins, like a base runner sliding into home plate.

His slide was long and fast, and he almost made it. But suddenly, a slot machine ahead and to the left burst open, showering coins in every direction. The jock floor manager came tumbling through the gash and immediately sprang into a defensive crouch, facing JB and blocking the exit.

JB skidded to a stop and froze, his gaze locked on the brilliant sapphire eyes. He could hear the others coming from all sides and knew that they would soon be upon him. And that left him with only one option. He would have to get by the floor manager who'd morphed into the creature crouched before him. While the rational part of his brain understood that this snarling man-beast with the shining eyes was no more real than the Shangri-La itself, the *irrational* part of his brain still needed convincing—and believe me, for someone as creative and imaginative as JB, that's a tall order.

He almost lost it right there, and he most certainly would have drowned in the world that I had created—and in doing so, left me in complete control of our body—but something clicked in his part of our mind just then, and he made the only winning move he could. Instead of *resisting* the fantasy, he *embraced* it. With every fiber of his being, he embraced it.

JB squared his stance and looked deep into those sapphire eyes—which, as expected, drew a vicious snarl of rage from the floor manager. But as he sprang, teeth bared and angled for JB's throat, a hand suddenly shot in between the two of them and gripped the floor manager by the throat. The floor manager's sapphire eyes went wide with shock as he stared into the stern gaze of JT the dealer, who had appeared out of nowhere at JB's behest. In a flash, JT the dealer pitched the floor manager like a rag doll into the row of slot machines. It was a deftly executed defensive move, but he didn't follow it up with any theatrics. And he didn't smile and wink at JB like it was all good, either. Because it wasn't all good. JB was still in danger, and JT the dealer was not there to provide him with amusement. He was there for one purpose only: to make the ultimate sacrifice.

As the wall of slot machines exploded and the ravenous creatures came rushing through, JT said, "Go—and don't look back."

JB opened the door and stepped across the threshold, but despite the dealer's warning, he couldn't resist taking one last look back. What he saw was both astonishing and horrifying at once. JT stood tall, blocking the way to the exit, as the vicious horde of fast encroaching creatures descended upon him.

Of course, it was only a fantasy, but it stung just the same. And for the first time in his life, JB felt real anger without any prodding from yours truly . . . which made perfect sense, considering that his anger was directed at *me* (which, I suppose, when you think about it, is sort of like JB being angry at himself, but let's not go there).

He wasn't angry at me for setting that hungry pack of creatures on poor old JT. It's not like it was really *my* fault anyway. I mean, after all, it was *JB* himself who'd called the valiant dealer to the rescue in the first place. Had he simply manned-up and faced those vicious creatures on his own, JT would still be back at the poker table with Marilyn, most likely sipping drinks and getting her number by now. And anyway, it wasn't like it was the *real* JT getting torn to shreds back there in the Shangri-La, because the Shangri-La, along with all of its inhabitants, was simply a product of JB's imagination (as designed and directed by me, of course), so *none* of it was really real.

He wasn't even angry that my ulterior motivation for setting up this little road trip in the first place was to get him alone so that I could wrest control of our body from him (he actually expects that sort of thing out of me—I'm an *id*, after all; it's in my nature to crave control and cause trouble, and at some level, I suppose JB has always understood this).

What *did* anger him was when I'd held that doorknob and kept him locked away from the secret room of memories inside our mind. *That*, he could not tolerate. It was like the time his cousin had locked him in the toy box. Or when Nick had locked him in the casket at the funeral home. JB doesn't like being trapped—inside or out. He just can't take it.

But what made it worse—*infinitely* worse—was that the one who had locked him up here in the Shangri-La happened to be his most trusted confidant. Me.

When he'd been trapped in both the toy box and the coffin, I had been right there sweating it out with him. But this time was different. This time, *I* was the one who'd closed the proverbial lid on him and held it shut while he struggled to escape. I suppose if I'd been using some small portion of our brain—the part that's capable of separating good ideas from bad ones, for instance—instead of just barreling at the situation head-on (as *ids* often do, even clever ones like me), I would have just opened that secret door to our memories and let him stroll right in, never to return . . . just let him live there in that soothing world, while I went on to take the reins in the here and now.

Hindsight. Everything is always much clearer in hindsight.

Anyway, JB was pissed at me, and I was pissed that my grand scheme had failed (particularly after all the preparation and work I'd put into it), and neither of us was ready to give an inch. We were at an impasse, plain and simple, and so what happened next, as crazy as it seems, was almost inevitable . . .

JB turned from the huge double exit doors of the Shangri-La to find that he was standing inside a little coffee shop. It was a quiet place with ambient lighting and a pleasant décor. Most of the booths along the wide front window were occupied by couples, while all of the active tables on the main floor were occupied by parties of three or more—all save for one. It was in the center of the shop, and it was the only table with a single occupant: a lean man in an expensive-looking dark suit and tasteful silver tie. His black hair was neatly combed backed to reveal his drawn countenance and blade-like nose. He had the sort of face that was difficult to pair with an exact age, but if JB had to guess, he would have pegged the man at fifty-something. With his solemn demeanor yet sympathetic eyes, the man looked like a funeral director. On the table before him was a cup of coffee and a slice of cherry pie whose flaky crust crumbled enticingly as he cut into it with his fork. JB stood frozen, unable to tear his gaze from the man. He had never seen anyone eat so slowly, each bite taken at a leisurely pace as if time was of no concern—as if the world had stopped spinning and would patiently wait to resume its business until after the last bite was gone.

The man had consumed less than a quarter of the pie slice when he set his fork carefully on the edge of the plate and reached for the steaming cup of coffee next to the creamer. He took a modest sip, set the cup back on the table, dabbed one corner of his mouth with a napkin, and spoke without looking up. "If you would care to join me, Justin, please do." He paused and then added, "Your friend is welcome as well."

JB and I both understood that the "friend" the man was referring to was me. I was dubious about the offer—there was something about the guy that I just couldn't cotton to. But JB liked his gentle demeanor, and before I could stop him, he stepped forward and took the seat opposite our new acquaintance. At a distance, JB had thought the man's eyes were blue, but up close, their color appeared to change with each minute shift of the surrounding light. They were kind eyes, tinged with a hint of sadness, the eyes of someone who has lived a long life and seen a lot of things. I didn't trust the man or his eyes, so I retreated back to my corner of our consciousness but kept vigilant.

The man addressed a passing waitress. "Excuse me, Mary. Would you be kind enough to bring my young friend here a slice of pie and a glass of milk?"

The waitress smiled and said, "Would that be the cherry pie?"

"Without question," said the man with a pleasant smile of his own.

"Coming right up, darlin."

"Thank you, love." The man turned his attention back to his plate and said, "The pie here is delicious. You shouldn't be afraid to indulge while you're young and the body is still forgiving. When you get a little older, you'll be surprised at what the body will no longer tolerate."

JB said, "You don't look that old."

The man smiled that sad smile of his again and said, "You're very kind." He paused and added, "But there's no shame in young eyes seeing the truth for what it is."

JB's cheeks flushed with a sudden sensation of guilt, and his heart ached as an old memory came flooding back into our consciousness. His grandmother had taken his mom and him out for brunch, and from his place at their table, JB could see this elderly woman with a severely hunched posture eating all alone at a table by the window. It was late spring, and the sun was shining through the window so brightly that the old woman's skin looked nearly translucent. JB couldn't have been any older than seven at the time, but he knew that other boys his age would have laughed at this old woman eating alone and made fun of her skin and the way her back was all hunched over—so badly, in fact, that it took tremendous effort just for her to lift the spoon to her mouth.

But JB didn't laugh at her, because to him there was nothing funny about a woman so old and bent over that it was difficult for her to lift a spoon to her mouth. As he sat in that restaurant, he wanted so badly to ask his mom if he could go over and sit with the old lady so she wouldn't have to be alone. But he didn't ask. He didn't know why, but he was afraid to ask, and so he just sat there, feeling sad for the old lady and ashamed of himself for not having the courage to ask his mom if he could go over to her table and keep her company. On their way out, they passed by the old woman's table. She looked up and smiled when she saw JB, and he smiled in return, hoping that she wouldn't see the sadness in his eyes. And later that night in bed, with the image of the old woman still on his mind, he cried himself to sleep.

JB was still thinking of this old memory when the man set his fork on his plate again, took another sip of coffee, and said gently, "She passed peacefully in her sleep at eleven thirty-six P.M. on the twenty-eighth of April, two-thousand and one. If it's any consolation, her last thought was of the little boy who'd smiled at her in the restaurant that morning."

I could feel JB's eyes starting to mist over, and I steeled his nerves from within. This man in the dark suit, with his calm demeanor and pleasant voice and sad eyes that changed color with the shifting of his mood (it wasn't a trick of the light, they actually changed color with his *mood*), was starting to grate on my nerves. He was trying to work on JB's emotions, and I thought it was a pretty dick move. But still, the guy kind of spooked me and so I kept my distance (I mean, come on, the guy was spouting off death dates and last thoughts, which is some crazy guru shit, and he could see me, or at least *sense* my presence inside JB, and he had eyes that changed color with his *mood*, for creep's sake—now tell me that *you* wouldn't be at least a *little* leery of that).

The waitress came with the pie and a tall glass of milk for JB, and old Silver Tongued Dapper Dan, with his freaky eyes suddenly shifting to a warm blue, oozed out a silky "Thank you, Mary" before turning his attention back to his plate. They ate in silence, the two of them, and JB tried to eat slowly, but he was so hungry after not eating all day that he cleaned his plate and drained his glass of milk before the Professor was even halfway through his own slice of pie. This didn't seem to bother the old guy; in fact, he looked pleased that JB had enjoyed the pie as much if not more than he himself. When JB smiled demurely, the Professor returned the smile, like a kindly uncle. But still, there was something in those strange eyes of his that gave me the feeling he was probing JB's eyes for any sign of me lingering back there.

I'll be perfectly honest here. Some people just don't like me (as evidenced by that petition to have JB deported or any of the other myriad nasty comments on threads from Facebook to YouTube to IMDb). But then, none of them really *know* me— or JB, for that matter. Most just take all the bad stuff they hear and run with it. I'm not saying I blame them for that—I've certainly provided more than enough fodder for the world to chew on, including but not limited to the "controversial" statement JB made at the Anne Frank house. (I just couldn't resist nudging him into *that* one. Who knew everyone would be so sensitive about it? And can anyone say with any certainty that the girl *wouldn't* have been a Belieber?) Or when he compared himself to Kurt Cobain. (Again, my bad. But in my defense, I *did* warn him that if he ever *repeated* it to anyone, they'd crucify him.)

There are also people very close to JB who don't like me

either. Now I'm not saying they're *wrong* for feeling the way they do—like I've said before, I am not one of those delusional *ids* who goes about blindly doing his thing, oblivious to the consequences. I know what I've done, and I'm not going to insult anyone's intelligence by denying any of it. When JB was little, I used to get up to all *sorts* of mischief (this was before I'd developed my sweet swaggy stealth moves), and all it took to shut me down was a line like, "You know better than that. Where's that sweet boy I used to know?" The moment his mom or grandmother pulled that line on him, I was done for—shot straight down the old hole and back into the abyss with one gulp of his mortified humility—and sometimes it would take *months* before I was able to crawl my way back to the surface. JB's conscience can be much more powerful than you'd think. Trust me, I've been smacked down by it enough times to know.

But the vibe oozing off of old Professor Freaky Eyes across the table from us felt a bit more chilly than mere dislike. I got the distinct impression that if I were to attempt pulling any of my sweet stealthy swagalicious moves on *him*, he'd have no compunction about breaking me in half like a twig and using the splinters to pick the pie crumbs out of his teeth. And he'd probably do it just as casually as he would brush a speck of lint from the lapel of his suit jacket. I could barely stand the sight of him, but I've got to admit, he impressed the hell out of me, the smooth prick—even the way he set his fork on his plate was awe-inspiring.

He stopped eating and set his fork on his plate (see what I mean?), and after taking another sip of coffee, he looked into JB's eyes and said, "I'm going to speak to you in French for a moment because the woman sitting at the table directly behind me has been listening to us, and I believe she's a bit worried there's something untoward in a young boy like you sitting with an older man like me."

JB shot a glance over the Professor's shoulder just in time to see the woman in question shift uncomfortably in her seat while clearing her throat. Then he turned his attention back to our new best friend, who proceeded in French.

"The young man in the far corner booth with the haunted eyes and pained expression is contemplating suicide," he said in a detached tone, his eyes shifting to a neutral shade of grey. "A string of impulsive bets has put him in a precarious position. Now when he sees something on which all signs point to 'go,' he hesitates and watches as his feelings turn out to be correct. And this has proven even more disconcerting than all the bets he's lost—knowing in his gut that the time to strike is at hand but lacking the courage of his convictions to follow through . . . "

He paused briefly here as the woman who'd been listening in from the table behind him got up with her kids and made a hasty exit. Then, without the slightest shift in his neutral grey gaze, he switched smoothly from French back to English and continued calmly with his story about the edgy young guy in the corner booth.

"He's going to reach the breaking point tonight—at the roulette table. He's going to place every last dollar he has on Black 11. And this will prove to be a very fortuitous decision, because indeed the pill will find the pocket of Black 11, and he's going to win a lot of money—all that he's lost thus far, plus a tidy sum in profit. But it's important to understand that he won't be happy—not in any meaningful sense of the word—because this will only be a temporary victory for him. He'll leave for home, his winnings secure in his pocket. But one day he'll return. In a month, perhaps, or possibly even a year—one never knows for certain with these sorts of things. But what *is* a certainty is that one day this young man with the haunted eyes and pained expression will eventually be right back where he is now, contemplating the same dire thoughts . . . and possibly following through on them . . . barring another lucky spin of the roulette wheel, or a fortuitous roll of the dice. And this is because it is in his nature to blindly follow through on sudden impulses rather than patiently wait for his better angels to show him the best path. You see, Justin, there are all sorts of paths—many which offer immediate gratification, but few that lead to sustainable satisfaction."

JB remained still and silent, like a model student in awe of his teacher. You'd have thought he was sitting there listening to Bob Dylan or John Lennon wax poetic over the meaning of life or some shit! I swear, it was all I could do to hold my tongue—or, more accurately, my urge to use *JB's* tongue and let loose with some prime verbiage Kid Swaggy-style. If you've seen those deposition tapes where that smug pencil-necked attorney kept going after JB with all those ridiculous questions, like "Do you know Raymond Usher IV?" and meaningless crap like that, then you know what I'm talking about.

But, like I said, I kept it zipped. This coffee shop guy was definitely *not* some pencil-necked attorney. For all his soft-talk and proper etiquette, you got the feeling he wouldn't just sit there and take some smart-ass punk getting all up in his shizzness, if you know what I mean. You got the feeling that if push came to shove, he'd sooner grab you by the scruff and barehanded bitch-slap you—or worse. You could almost see it in those calm, spooky color-changing eyes of his. It's always the calm ones you have to worry about. The calmer they are, the more volatile the explosion when you test the limits of their last nerve, believe me. So I just stuck to my little corner of our consciousness and kept it shut—I didn't have anything to prove to that uppity snob anyway.

For a change, JB was a little more daring than yours truly, and he asked a question that I'm not going to pretend wasn't gnawing at me as well. His tone was soft and respectful, and he looked the man directly in the eye when he asked: "Are you God?"

There was no guile in the Professor's eyes when he replied simply: "Which one?"

JB didn't expect that response (like so many people of faith, he has always blindly followed his own, believing it to be the "one true faith"). Confusion crept into his eyes, and for a while it was quiet again.

Then the Professor took a sip of coffee and said, "There are simple explanations, and there are more . . . complex ones. For the ease of understanding, I believe it's best we stick with the simple answers, if that's acceptable to you, Justin." The color of his eyes shifted from grey to pale blue, and he asked: "Do you mind that I address you as 'Justin?'"

JB shook his head; he didn't mind.

The man said kindly, "I've always felt it polite to address one by one's given name. And I've never been very good at playing games of subterfuge." He offered a small smile, along with a scarcely perceptible wink that I'm sure JB didn't catch. I could feel his gaze penetrating JB's eyes and homing in on my private corner of our consciousness, as if the "games of subterfuge" line was meant exclusively for me, and I thought *Touché* but didn't say it. I just held my position, crouched back as far as I could get in JB's consciousness, and eventually the probing gaze retreated and returned to JB.

"But as I was saying," he went on, "there is a path to everyone's destination. Indeed, there are many paths to all sorts of destinations, and one may pick as one pleases—I suppose this might be translated into your own religion's notion of 'free will,' if it makes it easier for you to comprehend. And this freedom to choose one's own path is precisely what it sounds like: the right to guide one's own destiny by the choices one makes . . . or doesn't make."

He paused and smiled that sad smile of his as he read the burning question behind JB's eyes. You could tell that he didn't want to dash JB's hopes, but he also wasn't about to lie to the kid just to save his feelings.

The pale blue of his eyes deepened, like the sky on a cloudless day, and he said, "I didn't give you life—that too fell into the category of 'free will choices made by others,' namely your parents—but I was there when you were born. And I was there when you were born into your 'second life' too—the same in which you currently live. And I was there for every moment in between, and every moment thereafter as well. I was there when you laced up your first pair of skates, and when you laid your stick to the ice for the very first time. I was there when you recorded your first video for Youtube. I was there every night you lay beneath the stars, gazing into the future and dreaming of a different life . . . "

In a flash, I took control of JB's hand, balled it into a fist, and slammed it on the table as I glared at him straight through JB's eyes. It was too much. He had no right to trespass on *that* ground. Not *there*. Anywhere else but there. He had *no right*.

I'd half expected him to rise from his seat and grow ten feet tall, eyes all ablaze, voice booming, like the grey wizard in that *Lord of the Rings* movie (you know, the scene where the old hobbit tells the wizard that he won't give up the ring of power). But he remained seated. It wasn't like my sudden outburst had scared him or anything—this guy wasn't afraid of jack squat. In fact, he looked almost serene, like a patient adult who'd seen worse temper tantrums and was simply waiting for the inevitable "receding of the tide." The guy had ice water in his veins, I'm telling you—Samuel L. Jackson would have backed down under the pressure of that chilly color-shifting gaze.

I retreated, but I was still giving him the old hairy eyeball from my place at the back of JB's mind. I was still shooting the old daggers at him because you don't mess with somebody like that, prying into their private moments and shit like that. You don't disrespect somebody like that and then stick it in their face. That ain't cool, that ain't swaggy. Even if you *are* a god, that ain't cool.

It was quiet again. Then Mr. Eye In The Sky said, "There are those who believe that in order to fashion a subject to one's liking, one must first break the spirit and rebuild it in one's own image. And if violence is necessary to achieve this end, so be it." He paused briefly before going on. "I am not strictly averse to aggressive action—it is sometimes an inevitable necessity—though temperance is always preferable. The only question to be asked is this: Is the prize that you seek worth the effort? If all you desire is control of the physical shell, I can assure you there's little reward in it because all of this . . . " He gestured to JB's body with a facile hand. " . . . is a temporary illusion."

He looked deeply into JB's eyes and caught sight of me crouched like a defensive animal in the corner. His gaze softened briefly, as if he felt something close to sympathy for me, and he said softly, "I too was once young and beautiful, with throngs of adoring fans hanging on my every word—not nearly as many as you have on your Twitter feed, of course, but then, the population was considerably smaller back in my day." The shadow of a sad smile appeared at one corner of his mouth, then disappeared. "It was a glorious time. But eventually, it passed, as all things do. Others, much younger and more alluring than I, rose seemingly from nowhere, and my 'fan base' diminished—though I still have a few . . . faithful followers." He smiled briefly again before reverting to his passive expression. "All things pass. Sometimes slowly—even gracefully, if you're lucky—sometimes in a heartbeat . . . a single fragile breath expelled without a moment's notice. And when that illustrious shell fades—and it will—what you're left with is what's on the inside. Cliché but true." He looked deeply into JB's eyes and spoke directly to me one last time: "I understand this isn't what you want to hear, but I'm not very good at telling stories with happy endings. In any case, you have my sympathies."

Then, without another word, the man went back to eating his pie, and as our table fell into silence, the ambient sounds of the coffee shop returned—customers chatting softly around us, the faint underscore of forks and knives on plates, the soft dripping of a coffee maker behind the service counter, the clinking of glassware in bus trays; nothing more.

My nerve returned shortly, and I was gearing up to tell

143

JB that it was time for us to go. I was prepared to take control and force the issue if necessary—anything to get away from Professor Freaky Eyes with his pious 'tude and lame parables. I'd had enough of that crap to last a *million* lifetimes, and I didn't want him poisoning JB's mind with any more of his spook stories about fading youth and short-lived fame. What a *complete* load! Look at Mick Jagger—he's like a hundred, and he still packs them in wherever he plays! Who the hell did this guy think he was kidding anyway? JB's only chance of survival in the spotlight was *me*. *I* was the one who got us to the top, and I was the one with the stones and the where-withal to *keep* us there! The sheer gall of this smooth-talking, pie-eating, shifty-eyed son of a bitch *really* got under my skin. I needed to get out and get some air, so I could think clearly and start working on a plan to get JB's head screwed back on in the right direction.

I was ready to do just that when Mr. Chew's Every Damn Bite As Slow As He Damn Well Pleases finally swallowed the forkful of pie he'd been chewing on forever, took another sip of coffee, and said calmly yet pointedly, "I believe the two of you have some things to work out. Perhaps it would be best to take it outside."

JB's eyes narrowed in confusion. When the Professor looked up to meet his gaze, I could tell that what he had to say was for JB alone. His tone was even more gentle than before, and you could see that he was trying to work some more of his guru mind-screw on poor old JB (which was pretty stupid because he *knew* I could hear anything that came through JB's ears—it was like when somebody wants to be a dick and starts saying something to someone else, knowing that you can hear every word of it, and that really bugs the crap out of me).

He said, "You need to understand that what I'm about to do for you is only temporary. The *id* is inextricably attached to the host, and thus, it would be impossible to permanently excise it without causing irreparable damage to the host . . . "

I was a little insulted at being referred to as "the *id*" and "it," as if I were some hideous growth that had suddenly sprouted on JB's perfect little muffin ass overnight—I *have* feelings, y'know? But I was more intrigued by the Professor's proposal, so I kept it tight and listened.

"But," he went on, "a brief *separation* of the host and *id* *is* possible without causing permanent damage. And it might even do some good." He paused and added with a measure of gravity, "One caveat: You must understand that once you step out that door, you will be on your own. I cannot intervene until the two of you have worked things out. And whichever emerges the victor shall have complete control of your body. Do you understand this, Justin?"

It was clear just whose side the Professor was on, but I didn't care. Only two things that he'd said mattered to me: First and foremost, once we stepped outside, JB was on his own, without any help from his smooth-talking, pie-munching savior; and, even better, whichever of us emerged the winner would get control of JB's body . . . and I was going to make damn sure that the winner would be *me*.

I was surprised when JB accepted the terms and got up—I'd actually thought for a second there that I might have to drag him out of the shop. I *did* give him a little nudge, though—just a tiny one—but as we started for the double doors at the far end of the coffee shop, the Professor spoke again, without looking up as he cut another measly portion from his slice of pie.

"I believe you might want to use the *front* exit, Justin," he said in that infuriatingly calm tone of his. "The one you're headed towards now will only take you back into the Shangri-La . . . and I don't expect that's a place you're keen to revisit."

I could have bashed his head in right there, I swear it. But instead, I just turned right along with JB and headed for the front door that let out onto the Strip. There was no need to worry. It was all good. I was about to get everything I'd ever wanted. I was about to have my dream come true, and it didn't matter if it happened inside the old Shangri-La or outside on the Vegas Strip. I was about to rise up in victory, and JB was about to go down. Oh, I'd *try* to save whatever part of him I could. I'm not a *complete* monster. I *have* feelings for the kid— he's like a *brother* to me, for shit's sake. But if it meant his total annihilation, then so be it. It was finally *my* time, and I wasn't about to lose, because losing just ain't Swaggy's style, yo.

The Strip was silent and deserted. No cars, no sounds, no people. Just the two of us, JB and I. And when I say the two of us, I mean the *two* of us. Though we'd left the coffee shop as one, we stepped out onto the Strip as two separate yet identical people . . . and on opposite sides of the street (however *that* worked out, I do not know, but I was starting to gain some genuine appreciation for old Mr. Merlin inside the coffee shop—I still thought he was a dick and all, but I had to admit that he was a pretty *impressive* dick, pulling off a stunt like this, I *had* to give him credit on that score).

The first thing I noticed as I stood on my side of the street was how liberating it felt to be inside my very own body. Just me. All by myself and in complete control. I paused for a moment to double-check, listening for any "outside" thought-waves passing through my brain. Then I dove deeper, probing the landscape of my cerebrum in search of that familiar hum of JB's generally docile and good-natured train of thought. I combed every inch—every curving crevice and hidden corner—but there was no sign of JB. Nothing but pure silence. I couldn't even find a sign of Lil E (who, granted, is pretty much silent *all* the time but usually can be found when I need a little refresher course in diplomacy). The whole of my brain was like a vast playground spread out for me and me alone. And the temperature was perfect—nice and frosty on one side while raging like a wildfire on the other. Because all you really need in life is the ability to freeze things out or set them on fire. Anything in between is strictly for whiners and good samaritans—neither of which anyone has ever accused yours truly of being.

I was still marveling at my new "single occupancy thinking unit" when I caught sight of my reflection in the front window of the Flamingo—a classic casino built by guys just like me, tough guys who took no shit off of nobody (of course, this wasn't the *original* Flamingo I was standing in front of, but it's the sentiment that counts, and that's good enough for me).

Anyway, so there I am, looking at my reflection in this window, and that's when I notice how swagaliciously buff I look. I mean, not to sound like a complete narcissistic douche, but I look *hot*. I've got this white wife-beater on, and I'm all tight and toned and swagged out with fresh ink (my left arm is like fully sleeved in these wicked tattoos, just like it was in the vision I'd conjured for JB back at Madame Tussauds Wax Attraction the day before), and my hair is cut close on the sides and the back and swept up into this sweet swagged-up pompadour, and I can't take my eyes off of myself. And when I pull up my shirt to check under the hood, there's like even more wicked ink, and my abs are all tight and ripped, and I'm like over the moon—I shit you not, my swaggy brothers and sisters, I was over the moon!

I was still standing before the plate glass window of the Flamingo, admiring the new and improved me, when something flickered at my periphery (if not for this sudden distraction, I imagine I could have just stood there for all eternity, lost in that ghostly image that gazed back at me with equal fascination and adoration—there simply is no purer love than that which you feel for yourself, and anyone who tells you different is either a complete troll or full of shit).

I turned with a cool glare toward the source of the distraction and saw him. JB. He was no longer standing outside the coffee shop across the street. He was on *my* side of the street, thirty or forty feet down the block. He stood there with the hood of his sweatshirt up, his face partially cast in shadow, his gaze fixed on me in a way that I'd never seen before. His stance was different, too; it wasn't rigid or tense but poised and confident. I couldn't help but smile because, even though I was no longer able to hear his thoughts, I understood with complete clarity that he was not only ready but *willing* to fight me. It was a bit of a surprising revelation because, up until that very moment, I'd always just assumed that his fighting instinct came from me and that without my influence he wouldn't have much of an appetite for mixing it up.

Still, I had my doubts and believed that the whole poised and confident hard-eyed stance routine might just be a bit of the old bravado, and so I moved right in at a smooth and steady gait (with just a hint of the old swagger in my step), giving him my most swagalicious smile as I bridged the distance between us. He didn't move an inch, not even when I got within a couple of feet. He just stood there, gazing out at me from underneath the red hood, like one of those comic book superheroes, all high and mighty with stoic righteousness. I would have laughed, but I was saving that for when he was on the ground after I'd knocked out a couple of his perfect teeth. *Then* we'd see who the *real* stoical badass was. Then we'd see who was in *control*.

I stepped in swiftly and swung my fist like a hammer. But instead of connecting with his jaw, my fist simply cut through the open air, which surprised the hell out of me because I had the drop on him and there was no way he could have dodged that punch. But he *did* dodge it. And even more surprising (outright *shocking*, in fact) was that he came up from this evasive maneuver with a counterblow that caught me right in the gut. Had I known he was capable of such a feat, I would have steeled up the old rock hard abs to absorb the blow, which, I will not deny, knocked the wind out of me—who'd have thought the kid had it in him?

I recovered quickly and threw another punch. JB dodged this one too and countered with another lightning-fast blow, this time to my jaw. The sound it made was more like a slap than a punch, and *that* really got the old furnace fired up because nobody bitch-slaps Swaggy. Nobody.

I struck out fast and hard, and this time I connected, clipping him a good one on the left ear. But JB answered that single shot with *three* blows in rapid succession. The first two connected with my face, both sounding more like slaps than punches (either the dirty little pecker was actively trying to enrage me, or there was something ridiculously out of whack with the acoustics on the Strip). The third blow was the prize winner; it hit me square in the chest, with enough force to knock me five feet back and onto my ass.

I sprang up instantly and came at him again, but he countered every strike as if he knew what I was going to do even before *I* knew it. And this time he used his feet as well as his fists. He was like some crazy ninja warrior, making all these sweet swagalicious moves on me, and I was all like WTF! I mean, I'm telling you, I *know* this kid, and in all the years we'd been together, I'd never seen any sign that he could fight like this—not like some *Karate Kid* meets *The Matrix*, with a little *Crouching Tiger Hidden Dragon* action thrown in for good measure. Not JB. No way. That sneaky old slickster in the coffee shop must have done something when he separated us. He gave JB some special ninja power and left me to fend for myself, with only my dark temper and cunning guile to protect me. It *had* to be that. That pompous pie-eating philosopher had given JB all the power because he wanted JB to win. He'd cheated and given JB an insurmountable advantage. That dirty old slow-chewing, smooth-talking sanctimonious rat had rigged the game by giving JB some special skill . . . a skill that I did not possess . . . it *had* to be because there was no way—

Everything stopped at once, and for a second I felt as though I'd just woken from a dream and was suddenly able to see with perfect clarity. I was flat on the pavement—for the fifth time, no less—when it hit me like a speeding locomotive, or a ton of bricks, or a hammer to the skull (or whatever other stale metaphor you'd care to insert here).

The Professor hadn't given JB any special power at all!

JB was simply using the skills that he *already* possessed. Skills that *I* sorely lacked in . . . because all of the signals that told our body how to *make* those moves came from *his* part of our brain. He's always been "the talent" (I've never denied that), and I've always been "the driving force behind the talent," so there was hardly any reason for me to pay attention during all those grueling and sweaty training sessions, in which he had perfected all those sweet swaggy moves so that he would be able to execute them flawlessly on stage before a throng of screaming fans. I'm an *id*, not an artist. I have neither the time nor the patience for all that Justin Timberlake-Michael Jackson moonwalking ass-wiggling shoulder-rolling spinning-on-the-toes crap. It's just not in an *id's* nature to express himself artistically. The skills of the *id* tend more toward the gut than the heart, and performing a nice tune that you can tap your toe to (even a sweet swagalicious one) cannot begin to compare with the allure of more "aggressive activities" when it comes to quenching the insatiable thirst of the average *id*.

If you're looking to change the world, call an artist; if you're looking to *conquer* the world, call an *id*.

Anyway, so there I was, down on the pavement and looking up at JB, when the cold hard truth came crashing in on me. There was no way that I was going to win this battle by squaring off with him in a "conventional" fight. Though our physical strength was evenly matched (our bodies, after all, were identical—save for the swagalicious upgrade that mine had undergone with the sweet additional ink and added muscle), there was simply no way I was going to overcome those lightning-fast reflexes and kung-fu dance moves of his. I was in my own body now, with my own brain—completely free of the "better angels" of JB's suffocating conscience—and it was time that I used the assets of my brain: the dark temper and cunning guile that have always served me best. It was time to face up to the egregious error that I'd made and readjust accordingly. I had been attempting to go at him in a head-on fair fight. And now it was time to take off the gloves and get down in the mud.

JB was still standing there, poised and ready for my next move, but I didn't make the move he was expecting. Instead of attacking, I got up and ran.

I wasn't certain that he'd follow, but it didn't matter either way, because if he didn't come to find me, I most certainly would go find him . . . *after* I had acquired the proper means to show him what *real* power was . . . and how to wield it.

I found what I was looking for at the Strip Gun Club, which is located at the north end of the boulevard, within walking distance of the Sahara. I don't know how I got there as quickly as I did, but the place was as deserted as the rest of the Strip, and the door was conveniently wide open. The place was like a candy shop for recently liberated *ids* itching for retribution. But I didn't waste time taking the grand tour. I went straight for the submachine guns. I was tempted to take the Thompson M1921, which fires up to 1,500 rounds per minute, but I opted for the Uzi 9mm, instead. It only fires 600 rounds per minute, but it's fully automatic and fits nicely in one hand—and it *was* the weapon of choice of the Terminator in the original movie, and let's face it, there ain't no bigger badass than the original Terminator.

I was back out on the Strip and heading south at this smooth swaggy gait, my eyes scanning for any movement, as the dark sky rumbled overhead and the beautiful lights of the hotels shined like beacons to show me the way, which didn't end up being all that far. I stopped in front of the Bellagio, where the fountain was dancing to that song *Time to Say Goodbye,* and I smiled—not only at the sweet timing of the song but also because I knew that JB was waiting for me inside.

I strode past the fountain and crossed swiftly under the canopy of the main entrance. The lobby was deserted, and

I headed straight for the casino. I'd actually thought he was going to make me work for it, that he would be hiding someplace and make me come and find him. But I spotted him almost immediately and raised the Uzi.

The first spray of bullets would have taken him out, but his reflexes were incredibly sharp, and he dashed behind this row of slot machines. The bullets cut through the slot machines, sending shards of glass and metal flying everywhere, but the crafty little prick didn't even suffer so much as a splinter. He bolted from behind the slots and did this wild-ass somersault over the top of a blackjack table like he was one of those *Cirque du Soleil* acrobats. I fired another rapid burst but didn't even wing him.

Then he was bolting from spot to spot, ducking out of sight just in the nick of time as I let loose with the old Uzi, raining a destructive spray of bullets but missing him by mere inches every time. It was like some crazy-ass shooting gallery, where the target refuses to stay still long enough for you to hit it. He just kept appearing out of nowhere and disappearing just as fast, like a taunting little lightning bolt touching down in a flash and then vanishing just as quickly.

I'd emptied the first clip and was reloading the next when JB suddenly popped up from behind a nearby craps table and whipped out a sawed-off shotgun, which had been smartly concealed inside his hoodie. I just had time enough to realize that I'd made the same mistake the Terminator had made at the nightclub in the original movie. Only this wasn't a movie, and *I* wasn't a machine. I was a person, inside my very own body, made of flesh and blood.

A line from another movie suddenly popped into my head: *If it bleeds, we can kill it.* And for some reason I found this terribly funny. Then my eyes went wide, and I moved to take cover. But it was too late.

JB pumped the shotgun's slide fast and let me have it square in the chest.

The impact knocked me back, but incredibly I was still

standing. Before I could make a move, JB pumped the slide, ejecting the spent shell (which seemed to float from the shotgun's port in slow motion, just like in the movies), and then he let me have it again. He did this three times in a row, lightning-fast, and the final round knocked me on my back.

As I lay there gasping for breath, JB ducked out of sight and took cover again. I reached for my chest, fully expecting my hand to come up dripping with blood. But it didn't. And when I brought my fingers close to my nose and sniffed, the pungent odor of salt filled my senses, strong enough to draw a gag reflex. But there was no blood.

I sat up quickly. My chest still ached, but it was nothing compared to the throbbing inside my head, where the blood was racing and roiling. The dirty little poser didn't even have the nerve to kill me! He'd loaded the shotgun with rock salt, which, I'll admit, stung like a bitch, but I was still *alive*—which didn't bode well for old JB, because now I was *really* pissed. Had he just had the guts to put a gaping hole through my chest, I could have at least *respected* him. Hell, the way he'd gotten all the way up to the gun shop without me seeing him and then back down to this end of the Strip in time to set me up like that—now *that* was a stone-cold badass move you *had* to respect. But then, after all that swaggy Mission Impossible stealth, he goes and gives up his one chance to take me out once and for all? That shit just don't fly. That's the shit that makes Swaggy see red, and when Swaggy sees red, you *know* there's a shitstorm coming.

I got up and tore the tattered wife beater from my body. My chest was all red from the rock salt blasts, and it stung like the way paper cuts sting—you know, just enough pain to keep you in a ripe mood—but I ignored the stinging in my chest and picked up the Uzi with murder in my eyes.

I caught up with JB at the MGM Grand and wildly unloaded every clip I had, but he just kept rolling and twisting and somersaulting like some crazy acrobat, dodging every bullet. By the time my ammo ran out, the MGM looked like a war zone after a full-scale drone assault. But JB was still alive . . . and without a scratch on him.

By this point, my blood was running so hot, it felt like my body might explode at any moment. JB was still hiding from me, even though I was out of ammo, and this would have been the perfect time for him to come out and finish me off with his little bitch-ass jujitsu moves. Of course, when he'd pulled that crap on me outside on the Strip, I wasn't nearly as angry as I was now, so maybe that's why he was still in hiding. Maybe he was waiting for me to cool down enough that his little sissy slap fighting maneuvers would have an effect. If so, he was in for a long wait.

I've never felt as angry and frustrated as I did at that moment. My new body was shaking so fiercely with rage that for a second it felt like the walls of the casino were shaking right along with me . . . as if the sheer force of my anger was enough to rock the very foundation of the casino. It wasn't until I opened my mouth and let out this earsplitting roar that the reality of the situation came crashing in on me: the walls of the casino actually *were* shaking . . . and not due to some seismic activity beneath the Earth's crust; these violent tremors were emanating from *me*.

And that's when I caught sight of JB again.

He stood at the opposite end of the casino, exposed and unarmed. And his expression told me everything I needed to know (he has never been able to hide anything of significance from me for very long, and this time was no exception).

The tremor that I'd just caused by unleashing my rage was *real*.

And by the guilty look in JB's eyes, it was a safe bet that he'd known I possessed this ability (or at least suspected it) from the moment we'd stepped out of that coffee shop and locked eyes from opposites sides of the street. I suppose the Professor might have given JB the heads-up on the "special abilities" we would have at our disposal once our "separation" took place. And I suppose JB was hoping to keep this little tidbit of info to himself—at least long enough to see if we could work out our issues without resorting to drastic measures. But he really should have thought about that before he bitch-slapped me and unloaded four rounds of rock salt into my chest. I'm generally a lot better at *not* resorting to drastic measures *before* you piss me off so badly that I'm seeing red.

I would have taken the time to give him my best swaggy eat-shit-and-die grin, with a nice little razor-sharp wink, but I didn't want to give him the chance to pull one of his high-flying ninja escape moves. So without warning, my hand shot out, the flat of the palm pointed like a weapon, and before JB could dodge it, I channeled my anger straight down the length of my arm and shot a pulse wave of raw energy at him. The invisible blast hit him square in the chest and knocked him clear into the far wall. It was like some crazy Jedi shit! The sheer force of that raw power surging through me was the most amazing sensation I've ever felt. My arm was still tingling from it when JB started to get back up to his feet.

I didn't wait for him to recover, though. I hit him with another blast—only this time, instead of letting go at the moment of contact, I grasped him with the energy and tossed him like a rag doll toward the front end of the casino. The velocity was so powerful that he crashed through the doors of the high stakes baccarat room and tumbled over the top of the farthest table. I walked casually through the ruins of the main casino, but when I reached the shattered doorway and looked inside, there was no sign of JB.

For a second, I was worried that I might have killed him. I didn't want it to end that quickly—certainly not after a lifetime of having to put up with his holier-than-thou good boy conscience keeping me from living life to the fullest. I wanted retribution here, and I wanted it to last. I wanted payback for thirteen years of life in the shadows (that's minus the first three years when I had complete control and the subsequent two years with Lil E teaching me the art of "diplomacy," before old Super E showed up and screwed the whole shebang royally).

I wanted to force that sanctimonious goody-two-shoes crap of his straight down his throat and watch him choke on it.

Then I heard a soft groan coming from behind the overturned baccarat table at the far end of the room, and it was like music to my ears—like a sweet swaggy hip-hop jam that you could really twerk out to. And now I did take the time to grin and savor the moment.

I was ready to call out to him—to tell him that it was time to face the music and ask if he had any last requests—when the huge overturned baccarat table suddenly flipped up and over and came at me with the velocity of a cannonball fired at close range. It happened so suddenly that I was caught completely off guard—I was actually still grinning when the edge of the table slammed into my midsection and sent me sailing backward. This sudden "flight" didn't stop when my back slammed into the opposing wall—I just went crashing right through it and ended up landing in the lobby, with the huge baccarat table on top of me, pinning me to the floor.

JB came through the gaping tear in the wall. He looked serious, but he didn't look angry. There was none of the fire in his eyes that burned in my own. He looked down at me pinned under the table, like *he* was Thor and *I* was Loki. The pain and disappointment in his eyes made me see red all over again—*him* looking at *me* like I was the spoiled little brother trying to usurp his throne (okay, I *was* trying to usurp his throne, but still, it's not like he had to be a dick about it—just lower the hammer and crush my skull, but spare me the weepy brotherly love crap).

He reached out with one hand—I think he was going to lift the table and offer me a hand up, but I didn't give him the chance. I didn't have enough time to flip the table and mount a proper attack, so I reached out above my head and wrapped the far-reaching invisible grasp of my energy around the first thing I could get a hold of, which happened to be that huge golden lion statue in the center of the lobby. I ripped it from that circular marble pedestal it sat on and threw it at JB with all my might. He didn't try to dodge it like I thought he would. And he didn't get crushed by it like I hoped he would. Instead, he caught it in the grasp of his own energy and set it down as if the damn thing were some sacred relic. I suppose this was to show me that he wasn't about to respond in a destructive manner unless it was absolutely necessary, but the look in his eyes as he gently lowered that big golden cat to the floor was practically reverent, as if he cared more about that gaudy statue than he did about me!

Anyway, it gave me the time to flip the table at him and spring back up to my feet. He blocked the flying table with an almost effortless gesture, and I spun on him quickly, hoping to catch a nice down and dirty shot at his back. But his reflexes were incredible. In one swift movement, he pitched the baccarat table aside and spun around just in time to block the shot coming from *my* open palm with a counter shot from *his* open palm, like he was Obi-Wan Kenobi or some shit . . . and trust me, I know JB better than anyone, and he ain't no Obi-Wan Kenobi.

I gave him the old razor-edged stare, and he gave it right back to me. Then I shoved harder, sending a sweet swaggy pulse wave down my arm and through my outstretched palm. He responded with equal force, and the two waves of opposing energy collided at the center, locking us in an infuriatingly frustrating stalemate—at least for one of us, it was. Though we were both straining physically under the pressure, JB's temperament was chill . . . so chill in fact that for a second I thought he was going to say some corny shit like, "It doesn't have to be this way, bro." But he didn't. He just kept meeting my pulse wave of energy with equal intensity and maddening patience.

We were at an impasse, neither of us able to break through the other's defenses, because our strength was too evenly matched. But as alike as we were, there were still differences between us. There were things that I was willing to do that JB was not (the classic advantage of the villain over the hero . . . and I had no compunction about playing the role of the villain in this little scenario).

With that simple realization, I took it down a notch and let the force of JB's pulse wave drive me back a little. I even threw in a nice little wince to let him know that I was close to defeat (I can look quite pitiful and helpless when the need arises—many a female has offered a lap for JB to rest his head on for some hair stroking and TLC off of my adorable wounded puppy routine). As predicted, JB's gaze softened and the energy coming from his outstretched palm decreased . . . just enough to give me the edge I needed.

I let him have it then with a sudden surge of my full power, and he went flying back into the wall behind the concierge desk. I thought I had him pinned there for a moment, but then he shocked the hell out of me by doing something completely unexpected.

He raised *both* of his hands and gave me a massive *double* dose of the old pulse wave. It hit me like a sonic blast and sent me crashing through the main entrance doors. Glass exploded in every direction as my body was shot outside like a lopsided missile.

I didn't land on the street, though. The blast of that single shot had been powerful enough to send me sailing clear *across* the street—I would have likely kept on sailing all the way to the interstate, but luckily the hard façade of the Excalibur Hotel and Casino was there to "catch" me. I landed on my feet in a stealthy crouch (I was getting used to this whole supercharged body thing by now) and immediately stood up. In one swift movement, I realigned my back with an audible crack. Then I twisted my neck to the left and the right, with satisfying cracks, and shot a dark gaze at the MGM Grand across the street. I was pissed, but I was also impressed. It had never occurred to me that we could use *both* hands with that little pulse wave thingy. Live and learn, I guess.

I stepped into the street at the same time JB came from the

ruined entrance of the MGM. We stood there for a moment like two gunslingers waiting on the draw.

I'll spare you the blow-by-blow description of what came next—suffice it to say that scarcely a single structure was left intact by the time our conflict had reached its apex. And still, throughout the entire engagement, JB remained focused and calm . . . or at least as calm as you can be when your doppelgänger is hurtling pillars from Caesar's Palace at you, or trying to crush you between the toppling twin structures of the Wynn, or skewer you with the spire of the Stratosphere (when I'm in full rage mode, I'll use any weapon I can get my hands on).

I shit you not, the whole battle was like something out of one of those ridiculous Transformer movies (the mindless sequels—not the original, which was pretty badass), or some other over-bloated Hollywood crap-fest. Had I been sitting in a cinema watching the two of us, JB and me, up there on the silver screen, smashing our way along the Vegas Strip, destroying everything in sight, *I* would have rolled my eyes in disbelief. I mean, come on, my swaggy brothers and sisters, where's the drama in smashing things up? Where's the tension? I'm talking genuine heart-stopping tension here. I'm talking *true peril*, the kind where the outcome will leave the audience devastated if the hero doesn't prevail. Where's the emotional investment? I mean, two guys with superpowers trashing landmarks as easily as a couple of kids knocking down a wall of toy building blocks just isn't enough to keep me from yawning, you know? There has to be something at *stake*. There has to be something worth *saving*. Otherwise, it all just blurs into a meaningless jumble of mindless action. I mean, seriously, with JB and I as indestructible as Superman and General Zod, bouncing back up no matter how many times we slammed into buildings and shit, it was all beginning to feel like a pointless exercise, from which there couldn't possibly emerge a victor.

I was beginning to think that this was exactly what old Professor Freaky Eyes had intended for JB and me to discover all along: that neither of us could emerge the victor in this particular battle; that, like it or not, we were stuck with each other and would just have to find a way to work together in our shared body—a prospect th really depressed the shit out of me.

I was shaking my head, ready to chuck the whole thing and call it a day, when something incredible happened. Like a sudden ray of sunlight breaking on the bleak horizon, true drama—fraught with real peril—entered the picture.

There amidst the rubble at the south end of the Strip stood an angel-faced boy. He had appeared out of nowhere, dressed in his one-piece pajamas with the footies as if he'd stepped straight from his warm, safe bed to see what all the commotion was about. He was just a little guy with blond hair and soulful eyes. He couldn't have been any more than two and a half years old. At first glance, you would have sworn that this boy was JB as a small child. But JB and I both knew better. We knew *exactly* who this little guy was.

I was the first to react. A small devious grin curled at the corners of my mouth because I knew that this little boy standing alone and defenseless in his jammies at the far end of the Strip was one of the three people that JB cared about more than anything else in the world—the other two being his mother and his sister, of course. But the boy was the youngest and indeed the most perfect selection for the dramatic peril our conflict so sorely needed, so my hat was off to that cagey old smooth-talker from the coffee shop for giving JB and me the ultimate challenge at the climax.

As I stood there, soaking it in with this sweet swaggy grin spreading across my face, I couldn't help but recall the tagline from that old Terminator sequel: *One sent to destroy, the other sent to protect—the only question: which of them would reach him first?*

A sudden chill raced my spine, and by the look in JB's

eyes, I gathered he'd felt a similar sensation—but while my chill was of the delightful sort, JB's was of pure terror.

I made my move in a flash. I extended both of my palms and sent every ounce of the power within racing down my arms. I'd assumed that JB would attempt to make a preemptive move, but he was smarter than that. Even though we weren't currently sharing the same brain, he knew my thought process all too well. He knew that I wasn't aiming for the little boy. He knew that I was aiming for something which lay well beyond the Strip. Something huge for the finale. Time was of the essence, and he needed to get to the boy before I managed to pull off what would amount to the crowning achievement of our battle.

I grinned and shook my head as if to say, *Too late, bro. You'll never get to him in time.* And as if to confirm this, an explosive cracking sound echoed from the southeast like a violent thunderhead. The origin of this sonic explosion was over thirty miles away—Black Canyon, home of the Hoover Dam, to be precise—but JB knew he didn't have much time before the results of my "creative effort" came crashing into the south end of the strip where the little boy now stood, alone and unprotected.

JB took off running, and I chuckled—there really was no way he could make it all the way to the other end of the Strip in time . . . at least not on foot. My chuckle cut off instantly when I caught sight of what JB was running toward. There was a brand new shiny sportbike—a Ducati Diavel, no less— parked right there on the street (courtesy of our good friend in the coffee shop, no doubt, the cheating prick). As JB hopped on the bike and fired it up, I doubled the strength of the twin blasts coming out of my palms, and as I did so, I could *feel* the concrete center of the Hoover Dam tearing like a newspaper in my invisible grasp . . . and then the water came gushing forth in a massive wave, racing over the miles between the Dam and the Strip, smashing everything in its path. And as I pulled with all my might to draw the raging water closer, JB raced down the Strip on the Ducati, deftly dodging the debris in his path.

It all happened so quickly, like a dream on fast forward, and suddenly the boy was within JB's range. At my command, the raging water breached the south end of the Strip. JB twisted the Ducati's throttle, pushing it to its top speed. I pulled one hand back in a hard motion, shifting the flow of the water so that it would take the little boy from behind.

This was it. The sky was rolling with thunder. The impact was imminent. As the wall of water slammed over the far south end of the Strip, it began to pick up speed. And suddenly it was there, looming like a tsunami over the tiny boy, who turned to see it but scarcely had the time to register that he was doomed.

Then just as the wall curled over into its deathly arc, JB came tearing up on the bike and released the throttle as he slid sideways. The bike went shooting out from under him, toward the raging water, where it was swallowed in a flash. JB tumble-rolled across the pavement, caught the boy around the waist, and shielded him with his body as he thrust his free hand, palm open, toward the descending wall of water.

For a moment, time seemed to stand still, and I gazed at the sight before me in complete and utter disbelief.

JB had not only reached the kid in time, but he was successfully holding the towering wave back with *one* hand, while the other held the boy's head close to his chest in a feeble attempt to protect him. By the way his outstretched arm was shaking and the strained expression on his face, I gathered that JB wouldn't be able to hold out much longer before the wave swallowed both him and the kid as sweetly as it had that prissy little sportbike. And this was something I just had to witness up close.

I strolled down to the opposite end of the Strip at a leisurely gait. I was no longer applying pressure to coax the flow of the water; there really was no need to. Good old inertia had taken care of that quite nicely . . . but if it needed a little nudge at the end to finish things off, I would, of course, be more than happy to oblige.

When I reached the end of the strip, I looked down at JB, who was on his knees, still holding the boy close to his chest, still warding off the massive curling wall of water with one fiercely trembling outstretched hand. I stood above him as a king—as a *god*—and looked down upon him as mist from the massive wave pelted my face like chilly needles, tiny daggers, egging me on. The sound of the wave was so incredibly loud that I had to shout to be heard. I told JB to look at me, and when he turned his eyes up to mine, I could see genuine pain in them. He was down to his last ounce of strength, and still he wouldn't give in.

I shouted at full voice to be heard above the din of the powerful wave, "Did you think that you could beat me? Did you think that I would just lay down and take it? Did you think that I would let you throw away everything that I've worked for, everything that I've *built* in you? The fame, the money, the fans—did you think you did all of that by *yourself*? Did you really think I would just stand by and let you piss it all away? Did you think I'd let you *humiliate* us like that and get away with it? *Did you?*"

I swung a tightly clenched fist at his cheek, and the blow rocked his head. But it didn't sound like a normal punch. It sounded more like the crack of a bullwhip—or an open-handed slap. And my knuckles didn't sting from the impact. That's when I realized that JB hadn't been slapping me back when our fight began. He'd been using his fists—only it hadn't been his *fists* making contact with my face and body, but rather the energy pulses emanating *from* his fists, hence the slapping sound effect.

It was a strange sensation, striking someone without actually making physical contact—without feeling so much as a reciprocal tingle in your knuckles—but I got used to it quickly and punched him again. The blow was even harder than the first, but JB didn't lose his grip on the wave. He just turned his gaze back up to mine and held it there silently, stoically—an impressive display of valor that did nothing to calm my anger. Indeed it only served to fuel the fire within, and I punched him again. And again. And again.

Each blow came harder than the last, and the whole time I kept shouting, *"Did you think you could run away from me? Did you think I wouldn't take you down with me? Did you honestly think I wouldn't set the world on fire and watch it burn?"*

When I finally stopped, my heart was beating wildly, and my breath was coming in staggered waves. JB turned his gaze back up to me again. His face was bloody and bruised, and his outstretched arm was trembling so fiercely it looked ready to explode. But his resolve was unshaken, and his gaze was steady. He just *wouldn't* give in. All he had to do was admit defeat and hand over the crown. But the stubborn little prick just wouldn't let me have this *one* victory. And the kicker is, I almost admired him for it.

Almost.

I took a couple of steps back and shook my head. I was done. If he wanted to go under, let the wave collapse on him. Let him drown in his sanctimonious righteousness. The freak in the coffee shop had promised our body to the winner. I could learn the dance moves, and the golden vocal cords would be mine, right along with the rest of the package. I could go on without JB. No one would know the difference.

I turned and began to walk away—for some reason I was no longer in the mood to see him get swallowed up by the massive wave. And that's when he spoke for the first time since the whole fight had begun. His voice was so faint that at first I thought I hadn't heard him right, but then he repeated the statement, softly yet clearly.

He said, "He's your brother too."

I turned back to see the little boy, still held in JB's protective embrace. But his face was no longer buried against JB's chest. He was looking right at me with those haunting eyes of his, so very like JB's. Then he reached out to me, and though the distance between us was at least ten feet, I could feel his hand touching my cheek. Tiny fingers caressing my cheek, like they used to when he was still in diapers. And with this sensation came a sudden wave of images of this little boy: walking along the beach with JB and me, his tiny hand holding ours; up in our arms with his legs wrapped around our waist and his head resting on our shoulder; asleep in bed with his head resting on our chest; blowing out the candles on his second birthday last November.

And as these images came flooding in on me, an unexpected emotion—more powerful than any I've ever felt—surged forth . . . an emotion that I'd always thought was exclusive to JB, and certainly one that I would have never expected to encounter while in my own separate body.

I grinned bitterly through the sudden tears that welled in my eyes and thought, *Touché, you slick son of a bitch. Good job finding the defrost valve on the self-centered id's cold heart. Excellent setup. Well played, you dirty cheating rat savage. Hope you choke on that last slice of pie.*

But as angry as I felt at being set up by our coffee shop guru, I couldn't stop the wave of raw emotion that coursed through my body. I tried to tell myself to forget the brat and just take off, but the emotion—the *love*—that I felt for that little boy was suddenly suffocating all of my better demons. As a single tear fell, scalding my cheek, every selfish instinct within me was crushed right along with it . . . until all I could see, feel, taste, and breathe was an all-encompassing love for that tiny, helpless boy wrapped in his older brother's protective embrace . . . *my* embrace. (Now, do you understand why your typical *id* avoids any heartfelt emotion like the plague? It's a real downer, trust me.)

Don't get all worried. The kid didn't get swallowed by the big bad wave. He *almost* did—right along with JB and me—but I intervened just as JB's arm (or palm, or whatever it was that produced those wicked pulse waves) gave out.

I turned on the collapsing wall of water and, with one

hand, held it back. The only trouble was that it didn't recede. I'd thought since *I* was the one who'd summoned this wrath of Poseidon that naturally it would recede on *my* command, but it turns out once you get one of these water-wall tsunami things going, they pretty much develop a mind (or will, or whatever) of their own.

Anyway, I had to use just about every last drop of my power to fend off the big bastard. I swear, it was like that thing had a hard-on for JB and the kid, and it was really starting to piss me off. So, like any self-respecting *id* would do, I dug in and gave it the full thrust of my sweet swaggy pulse waves (while shouting every filthy word in the book at it) until finally, it receded.

It was probably more harrowing than I'm making it sound, but the whole thing was so exhausting, it wears me out just thinking about it.

Anyway, so once it was over, I just sort of collapsed right there on the Strip next to JB, all out of breath and drained in every way imaginable. I'm not going to lie to you—I was hoping that I would have enough energy left over to give JB a nice parting shot for putting us through all of this, to begin with, but I was as tapped as he was. It was all I could do just to lay there and breathe.

We were still lying there when old Socrates of the Strip came from the coffee shop in his expensive-looking funeral suit and tasteful silver tie and strode over to us. His expression, as usual, looked cool and composed as he surveyed the destruction with a casual eye. Then he looked down at us, JB and me, and spoke in that nauseatingly calm tone of his.

"If you're quite finished. I have a lot of work to do, putting all this back to right." He took a measured pause and then spoke directly to me. "That was a nice touch with the Hoover Dam. I hadn't expected that. A little more work for me, but a nice touch."

I'd have told him to bite me, but I was too exhausted to be a smart-ass—and to be completely honest, his calm eyes that changed colors with his mood still spooked me a little, so I kept my mouth shut.

He sighed this soundless sigh and then smiled warmly as he extended a hand to JB's kid brother (who surprisingly took it without reservation, as if the creepy old coot was a trusted member of the family—unbelievable!). Then with a glance down at JB and me, he said, "I have to get this little one back home now—it's well past his bedtime. I'll be back in short order. Please use the time I'm gone to resolve any remaining issues you may have."

And just like that, the smooth-talking, pie-eating coffee shop guru was gone, and JB's kid brother with him.

We lay there for a long while, JB and I, both of us silent.

Then finally JB said, "What do you want?"

His voice sounded flat, and I knew that he was in no mood for games, so I responded in earnest.

"You know what I want, bro."

JB didn't even blink; we both knew that he wasn't about to give in now, certainly not after all that I'd put him through over these past three days.

"What *else* do you want?" he said, just as flatly as before.

I thought about it for a moment and then said, "I want a tattoo—like the one that stoner at the party last night had . . . on the forearm, just below the crook . . . right there, bro."

I touched the inside of his left forearm, just below the crook, to show him where I meant, and he nodded.

It was only after I'd retracted my hand that something occurred to me: this was the first time I'd ever made physical contact with JB. Even when I was punching him during the heat of the battle, there hadn't been any skin on skin contact, because my fist had never made contact with his face; it was the energy pulsing *from* my fist that had caused all the damage. But when I'd reached out to show him where I wanted to put the new tattoo, I actually *touched* him, and for a moment there, I wished more than anything that he would touch me back—just a pat on the arm or a brotherly punch to the shoulder, or maybe even a fist bump. But he just lay there beside me, gazing up at the stars like he used to do when we were kids dreaming of the future.

It gave me a momentary warm rush, watching JB gaze upward like that. But even as I turned my own gaze toward those shimmering pinpoints of light in the dark sky above, I knew that everything had changed.

We weren't kids anymore. And we had already ascended well beyond those once distant stars.

DÉNOUEMENT

There really isn't much more to tell—nothing that you don't already know anyway . . . unless you spent the entire year of 2013 living in a cave with no TV and no Internet access, that is (let's face it, if JB's life were a movie, I would have easily snagged the MTV award for Breakthrough Performance of the Year—after all, I *did* make an undeniably indelible impression in 2013 . . . culminating in the swaggiest mugshot ever ;-)

I guess I could go on about the continuing struggle for power between JB and me—though, I believe that too has been well-documented and spread out nice and thick across the Web for any and all to see. And if you don't want to waste time surfing the Web for all the dirt on JB and me, you can always find a nice little condensed version of our trials and tribulations in any number of magazines—the March 15th, 2014 issue of *Rolling Stone* (#1204) comes readily to mind, with its full-cover image of JB, along with that irresistible title: *Bad Boy: Why JB Just Won't Behave*. It's not a crap article, actually, and it got most of its facts correct. It even offers up a remedy to what's ailing JB—a simple little career-saving move that JB could make to put everything back the way it was before all the shit hit the fan: Play the redemption card. Own up to the bad behavior, apologize, and promise to be a good boy from here on out.

I could tell you that this advice from the *Rolling Stone* article isn't all that far off the mark. I could tell you that all JB would have to do is stand up to me the way he did back on the Strip that night. Take me on with everything he's got. Rip up those thorny vines that have sprung from the seeds I'd planted back in Sin City. Take them in his bare hands, and never mind how they tear at the flesh—just rip them up by their roots and cast them aside.

He could do this in a heartbeat. He has the strength within to put a stop to all of my over-the-top antics and wildly outrageous behavior. And who knows? Maybe one day he'll do just that.

Of course, I won't go down without a fight—what self-respecting power-hungry *id* would? I'll claw and kick and scratch and bite until my last breath. And if I lose, I'll slink back and lick my wounds as always—we're survivors, we *ids*; we know how to bide our time until our skills are required by the host.

But for now, I don't want to think about all that. To be honest, it's a real downer, and I hate leaving things on a depressing note. So, I'll close this little tome with a more positive anecdote. I'm sure you're all curious about what happened anyway. But don't get too excited. It's not like it was some sweet-ass swagged-out palooza or anything like that. It was still a bit of a downer, but it was sort of sweet too. If you're the emotional type, get your hankies out; if you're a hardass, step off and get over yourself—even *I* was a little moved by this one.

We got back to our corner suite at the Aria shortly after midnight, and though we were both exhausted, JB did not collapse onto the bed. He went straight to the huge window and stood there for a long while, gazing out at the lights of the

Vegas Strip. All of the buildings we'd trashed now stood perfect, as if nothing had happened down there at all. The pillars of Caesar's Palace were back where they belonged; the gaudy golden lion façade once again framed the entrance of the MGM Grand; the spire of the Stratosphere pointed straight as an arrow toward the night sky. All had been restored to its former glory—including JB and me. Back in the same body. *His* body, free of all the extra swaggy ink and added muscle mass. Just JB.

As I gazed at him from my place in the window—a familiar ghostly reflection that used to provide strength and confidence when he needed it most—I noticed that the bloody scrapes and bruises I'd given him during our conflict down on the Strip were all gone. Everything had been put back to the way it was before the two of us had stepped out of that coffee shop in our own separate bodies. It was as if the past few hours had been erased.

But JB and I knew better. We both knew exactly what had happened, and neither of us was ever going to be able to forget it. We had crossed our own personal Rubicon (the point of no return), and things could never be the same again. Too many words had been said (most of them mine), too many irrevocable acts had been committed (again, most of them mine), the long trail of dominoes had begun to fall, and it was anybody's guess just where they would stop.

As JB stood in silence, I could feel the myriad raw emotions cascading and colliding within, and though the sensation was less than pleasant, it felt good to be home, back in the familiar body that we were meant to share.

Don't get me wrong. I still wanted *control* of our body, but I no longer had the desire to drive him out of it. I understood that I needed him, perhaps even more than he needed me, and this understanding scared me a little. Nobody wants to believe that they need someone more than that someone needs them. The truth is, I realized somewhere along the way that I genuinely like JB, and that I even respect him a little. The way he'd stood up to me in the heat of battle on the Strip, and the fact that he didn't lose his cool, no matter how rough things got— those are some admirable traits . . . and, as much as I hate to admit it, they're qualities I sometimes wish I could possess.

JB continued to gaze out the window for a while longer, his thoughts just out of my reach. Then he took out his wallet and found the dog-eared auto parts card the cabbie had given him a couple of days ago. He turned the card over and stared at the number the cabbie had written on the back as if debating the hardest decision of his life. He fished his phone out of his pocket, but still he hesitated.

I thought about giving him a nudge, but I knew better. I knew that it had to be *his* decision to return to our life back home. And even then, there still was no guarantee that he wouldn't throw in the towel and announce that he was retiring, or at least taking an extended break from the limelight. I had laid the seeds by giving him a glimpse of what life would be like *outside* of the golden circle of stardom, and now all I could do was sit back and wait to see if those seeds would take root.

I was still holding my breath when the cabbie's parting words to JB sounded off in our mind: *Stick this in your wallet. If you get into trouble, you call me, and I'll come on a hot dime. Don't matter what time it is, day or night, you call me, and I'll come get ya. You got that?*

That was all JB needed to get his fingers dialing.

When the phone rang for the sixth or seventh time, JB started having second thoughts, but something told him to hang in there, and after a few more rings, the cabbie's voice came through with, "It's your dime, shoot."

At the sound of that familiar gruff voice in his ear, a sudden wave of raw emotion swept over JB, and his own voice sounded terribly young and vulnerable when he said, "Eddie?"

Eddie said, "The one and only."

JB said, "It's me . . . the kid who looks like that Beaver kid . . . do you remember . . . ?"

The line went silent for a long moment, and JB closed his eyes tightly, praying that Eddie would remember. It had only been a few days ago that Eddie had driven him from Cali to Vegas, but it felt more like a lifetime—the sort that ravages the body and drains the soul, leaving nothing behind but a hollow shell—and suddenly JB wasn't sure of anything anymore.

Then Eddie's voice came through like the voice of an old acquaintance, "Sure I remember ya, kid. Are you all right?"

A hot tear spilled down JB's cheek, and he struggled to keep the emotion from breaking through. "Can you come get me, please . . . I want to come home now."

A woman's voice came from the background on Eddie's end. In a groggy tone, she asked Eddie who he was talking to. Eddie told her to pipe down and sleep it off. Then his voice was filled with concern as he asked JB if he was hurt, if anybody had tried to mess with him. JB scarcely choked out a "no." He tried to add that everything was fine, but he couldn't get the words out.

Eddie told him to stay put, that he was on his way and would be there in a "hot minute." And he wasn't kidding about that, because he pulled up to the Aria in his cab about ten minutes later (apparently, he'd picked up a fare in LA earlier that evening and drove her to her place just outside of Vegas; she must have enjoyed his banter because she'd invited him in for a drink, and the rest, as Eddie put it with a grin, was history).

JB was waiting on the curb, and when Eddie arrived, he got up and went straight to the cab without looking back.

Even as the lights of the Strip faded in the rear window, he didn't look back.

He only spoke once—when he asked Eddie if it would be all right to make a stop before they headed home. Eddie was completely cool about it. JB gave him the address, and a few minutes later they were parked across the street from the house with the familiar-looking battered Jeep sitting in the driveway. The light was on in the living room and the curtains stood open like the proscenium of a stage, and JB sat in the back seat of the cab watching the story inside that warmly lit space unfold.

Sitting on a short wooden stool in the middle of the living room was this eleven-year-old kid. JB recognized him at once from the picture Sandy the Guitar Center guy had shown him earlier that evening. It was Nick's kid brother, Braden, and he was playing his brand new Larrivee guitar and singing . . . words and music that JB could not hear, though he imagined it was one of his songs—*That Should Be Me*, or perhaps even a sweet acoustic version of *As Long As You Love Me*.

I could feel the swelling of JB's heart as he watched Braden's fingers move gracefully over the strings of that guitar. I could feel the tremor of a sad smile tugging at the corners of JB's mouth as the boy's shiny hair fell sweetly over his eyes. And I could feel the tears brimming as JB caught sight of Nick sitting back on the couch with a proud smile as he recorded his younger brother's performance with a video camera.

I don't know how long we stayed there watching that scene through the window, and I'm not sure exactly what JB was thinking—whether he was happy or afraid for the kid. But for me, it was like we'd discovered a porthole in the universe . . . one that took us back to that simple yet perfect place in time when JB was still a kid, and the dream was still worth dreaming.